BIGGLE

'Nellie Tomkins was twelve,' explained Detective-Inspector Gaskin of Scotland Yard. 'She was the only child of a couple who live in a cottage near Watton, in Hertfordshire . . . Last Monday she was walking home from school as usual when some devil hit her on top of the head and left her dying beside the road. In a matter of minutes she was seen and picked up by a passing motorist. By the time they'd got her to hospital she was dead. That's as much as we know.'

'No clue to the killer?'

'One. If you can call it a clue . . . A couple of yards from where the body was found lay a box of chocolates. . . .'

About the author

Captain W. E. Johns, who died in 1968 at the age of 75, served with considerable distinction in the R.F.C. in World War 1. After working with the R.A.F. in peacetime he became a prominent Air Correspondent and author of aviation books, and in 1932 he founded the magazine *Popular Flying*. Biggles first appeared in short stories in the same year, a character who was typical of the kind of man Captain Johns knew in the War.

Altogether Captain Johns wrote 85 books about Biggles, who has now become one of the most famous characters in children's fiction.

Biggles Investigates

Captain W. E. Johns

KNIGHT BOOKS
Hodder and Stoughton

Text copyright © Captain W. E. Johns 1964

First published in 1964 by Brockhampton Press Ltd
(now Hodder & Stoughton Children's Books)
First published in paperback 1970

Knight Books edition 1985

British Library C.I.P.

Johns, W.E. (William Earl)
   Biggles investigates.
   I. Title
   823'.912[J]   PZ7

   ISBN 0-340-10429-5

Printed and bound in Great Britain for Hodder and
Stoughton Paperbacks, a division of Hodder and
Stoughton Ltd., Mill Road, Dunton Green, Sevenoaks,
Kent (Editorial Office: 47 Bedford Square, London, WC1 3DP)
by Hunt Barnard Printing Ltd., Aylesbury, Bucks.

CONTENTS

Chapter 1   Biggles Investigates............................7

2   A Ring o' Roses 28

3   The Long Chase............................41

4   A Matter of Co-operation 66

5   Biggles Cracks a Nut 84

6   The Birthday Present 100

7   The Case of the Amateau Yachtsmen 111

8   The Boy Who Watched the Planes Go By 145

Chapter 1

BIGGLES INVESTIGATES

Air Commodore Raymond, Chief of the Air Police Section at Scotland Yard, looked up from his desk as, after a tap on the door, Biggles walked in.

'You sent for me, sir,' said Biggles.

'There's an aircraft lying on its back in a field near the village of Upgates, in Wiltshire,' stated the Air Commodore. 'I'd like you to go down and have a look at it. You'll find it on a farm called Fennels.'

Biggles looked mildly surprised. 'Is there something special about it, sir?'

'Very much so. It's a foreigner; a Spaniard, to be precise, if my information is correct.'

Biggles' eyebrows went higher. 'Spanish! Was it on an official visit?'

'No.'

'Then what the devil is it doing here?'

'That's what I'd like you to tell me. The Spanish government might be able to tell us, but that would take time.'

'What's the type?'

'I don't know. You should recognise it. Apparently it's a Spanish Air Force job. It wears military markings.'

'What has the pilot to say about it?'

'Nothing, for the simple reason that he can't be found.'

'He must have been lucky and got away with it. He shouldn't be hard to find. He can't be far away. Who found the crash?'

7

'The pilot of a Fleet Air Arm helicopter, on an early morning cross-country training flight, spotted it lying in a big field. He made a signal to his station, whereupon the ambulance was sent out. As nobody could be found it went home again. The station officer phoned the local police to put a guard on the machine and informed the Accidents Branch at the Air Ministry. They phoned me to see if I knew anything about it. If you want to see it you'd better hurry because the Inspector of Accidents is going down, so it won't be long before a breakdown party arrives to clear up the mess.'

'Do you happen to know the name of the man who owns the land on which the machine was found? I might want to have a word with him.'

'He's a sheep farmer named Diverton. His place is about two miles south of Upgates.'

'I'll slip along right away,' said Biggles. 'How on earth could a Spaniard have got here? Even a pupil on his first solo could hardly have lost his way to that extent. Last night was fair; practically no cloud.'

'I was thinking the same thing. But we must remember the aircraft was only found this morning, shortly after daybreak; for all we know it may have been lying there for some days.'

'That doesn't strike me as likely. Most farmers, or an employee, cover the ground at least once a day. However, I'll see what I can make of it.'

Biggles returned to his own office, where Police Pilot Bertie Lissie was alone on duty. 'There's an aircraft lying on its back in a field in Wiltshire. The Chief wants me to have a look at it. I shall fly down. If you feel like coming with me we can leave a chit for Ginger saying where we've gone. He should soon be in so he can hold the fort while we're away. Let's get along. I'll give you the gen, as much as is known so far, as we go.'

Less than two hours later an Air Police Auster was losing height as it circled over a low-wing monoplane, lying in a big pasture, showing the undersides of its wings. A man in police uniform was standing beside it.

Biggles landed, taxied close to the wreck, got out and made himself known to the constable, who must have had a sense of humour, for he remarked: 'This is a queer bird, sir. Never saw one with feathers this colour before.'

By 'feathers' he must have meant the red and yellow Spanish military ring markings.

Biggles agreed it was a rare specimen. 'Has anyone been here?' he enquired.

'Not since I came on.'

'How about Mr Diverton, who I believe owns this land? Hasn't he been over?'

'Not since I arrived. I called at the farm when I left my bike there, but his wife said he had gone to market. That's his house over there.' The officer pointed.

'I take it you're from Upgates?'

'That's right, sir.'

'What do you know about Mr Diverton?'

'Not much. Nice feller, what little I've seen of him. He hasn't been here long. Moved in last Michaelmas twelve-month. Keeps himself pretty much to himself.'

Biggles nodded and proceeded with his inspection of the aircraft, taking time over it.

'Am I right in guessing it's a Hispano D.1?' said Bertie, as they moved slowly round the machine, a two-seater.

'Dead right. It's classified, I believe, as an Advanced

9

Trainer. If my memory serves me it has a range of a bit over eight hundred miles, so it could have got here from Spain without an intermediate landing. The pilot was flying solo.'

'How do you know?'

'Look at the safety belts.'

The front one was hanging loose as if the pilot had unfastened it in order to drop out. The rear one was secured tightly across the seat showing it had not been used.

Biggles went on. 'I can't see a passenger, having got out, going to the trouble of refastening the belt.' By lying flat on his back he was able to get below the cockpit and examine it. He felt in the usual pocket in the instrument panel. Then he slithered out and stood up.

'Find anything?' queried Bertie.

'Nothing. Not a paper of any sort – not even a map.'

'That's a bit odd.'

'The whole thing's odd. In fact, I'd say there's something unnatural about it. If the pilot was able to walk away he must have been damn lucky, that's all I can say. Look at it. If the cowling hadn't been strong enough to take the weight of the machine he'd have been trapped. And that isn't all. Even if he wasn't hurt in the crash he could only have got out by dropping on his head.'

Bertie went on. 'He must have been ham-fisted. He had all the room in the world to get on the carpet, even with a groggy engine, yet he had to end up like this.'

'You've put your finger on something else that puzzles me,' declared Biggles. 'It takes something to turn a machine, even a small type like this, completely over on its back. Only by being brought to a sudden stop would it do that.'

'Jammed brakes, causing the wheels to seize up, would do it.'

'But the brakes aren't jammed.' Biggles reached up and spun a wheel to prove it. 'With plenty of room in front to run on there was no need to use brakes anyway. Had the machine come in at too steep and angle there would have been a real crack-up. The wheels would have buckled and the tyres burst. That didn't happen. This machine stopped with a jolt, yet there's practically no damage. I don't understand it.'

While speaking Biggles had gone to the front of the aircraft and was examining closely the undercarriage struts which, of course, were pointing to the sky. He looked again at each one in turn even more closely, a strange expression creeping over his face. He gazed across the field to the left, where it ended in a thickset hedge; then to the right, where it was bounded by an area of rough gorse and broom.

'I'll tell you something,' he said quietly. 'The man responsible for this knew something about war flying.'

Bertie looked astonished. 'How the deuce did you work that out?'

Biggles ignored the question. 'Come over here,' he said, walking towards the gorse. Reaching it he took a course roughly parallel with it, zigzagging, eyes on the ground.

'Are you looking for something?' asked Bertie, unnecessarily.

'Yes. You can help me to find it. Somewhere about here there could be a hole in the ground.'

'A hole? What sort of hole?'

'The sort of hole that would be made by a stake

11

having been driven well in.'

'Why here, particularly?'

'I'm working on the angle the machine is lying, assuming the pilot knew what he was doing when he tried to get down.'

Within a minute Bertie was saying: 'Here we are. Is this what we're looking for?' He pointed at the ground near his feet.

Biggles looked at the hole, about three inches in diameter. 'That's it. With a little patience we should be able to get this buttoned up. Now let's try over the other side.'

He walked right across the field, taking a line on the aircraft, to the hedge on the far side. 'See if you can find me another hole like the last one,' he requested. 'There may be several, but there should be one here.'

In less than five minutes they had found it – an identical hole.

'Would you mind telling me what all this is about?' asked Bertie, plaintively.

'Use your head. You can see what I can see. I don't know the answers yet; but I can tell you there's more to this than meets the eye.'

'Such as?'

'The machine lying over there was expected by someone on the ground, someone who didn't want it here and was prepared to do some dirty work to stop it. And, by thunder, that's just what he did.'

'Did what?'

'He stopped it.'

'Who stopped it?'

'Ah! That's the big question. Hello, here come the RAF boys to take over. I shall have to ask them to leave

12

the crash as it is for the time being. There's some evidence on it. It's time we had a word with Mr Diverton. According to the constable that's his house on the far side of the gorse bushes. You can just see the chimney. The machine lies on our way, so I'll have a word with the officer in charge of the working party as we go past.'

As the farm appeared when they had breasted a slight fold in the ground it was a small, fairly modern, very ordinary brick house, unattractive, with no outstanding feature, obviously having been built with economy as the first consideration. It was reached from some distant road by a narrow, muddy lane. There were the usual wooden barns and other outbuildings, and an odd tree here and there.

To reach the lane it was necessary to pass through the gorse bushes, about an acre of them; but this presented no difficulty, a well-worn sheep track which by-passed the thickest growths offering an easy route. Several times as they made their way through the thorny shrubs Biggles left the track to snatch a glance between them. Once he kicked up a loose turf, considered it for a moment and then replaced it. He said nothing.

They came to the nearest barn, between them and the house. It was a rather ramshackle structure of tarred boards with a corrugated iron roof. The double doors were shut. After a glance in the direction of the house Biggles opened one of them to reveal the usual clutter of farm implements, tools used for hedging and ditching and coils of sheep wire.

Still Biggles did not comment. They went on to strike the lane a little distance from the house just as a motor vehicle appeared round a bend. It turned out to be a baker's van, as a notice on the side of it proclaimed. They stood aside, close against a hedge that followed the lane, to allow it to go past.

'Stand still. I'd like to watch this,' said Biggles.

The van stopped at the door. The driver put some loaves in his basket and delivered them. A woman took in the bread but did not close the door. The baker's man returned to his van, put two more loaves in his basket and went back to the door, which was afterwards shut. The driver reversed his car, and would have continued on his way home had not Biggles raised a hand to stop him.

'How often do you deliver here?' enquired Biggles.

'Three times a week. Monday, Wednesday and Saturday,' was the reply.

'Thanks,' returned Biggles. 'That's all I wanted to know.'

The van went on its way.

To Bertie Biggles said: 'Let's try our luck at the house.'

They went to the door. Biggles knocked. It was opened by a dark-eyed, low-browed woman of middle age, dressed entirely in black, who, when she was younger, must have been strikingly handsome.

Biggles raised his hat. '*Buenos dias*,' he said politely.

'Buen —.' The woman broke off abruptly. 'What did you say?'

'I said good morning,' answered Biggles pleasantly. 'Is Mr Diverton at home?'

'No. He's away at market.'

'What time are you expecting him back?'

'Why?'

'I wanted to speak to him about the plane that crashed on his land.'

'I don't know when he'll be home.'

'Are you Mrs Diverton?'

'I am.'

'Is there another man in the house who might answer one or two questions?'

'There's no one else here.'

'Very well. I'll call back later.'

The door was closed.

Biggles walked back a little way along the lane, stopped, and took a seat on a fallen tree. 'This begins to add up,' he said quietly, as Bertie sat beside him.

'Mrs Diverton didn't say much.'

'She said enough. She's Spanish, so ruling out coincidence I'm pretty sure she's the hook-up with the plane. She knows all about it.'

'How do you know she's Spanish?'

'In the first place she looked it, every inch of her. I must admit I wasn't prepared for that. On the spur of the moment I tricked her into admitting it. As you must have noticed I said good morning in Spanish, and she, from sheer force of habit, started to answer in the same language. Then she thought better of it and switched to English. But it was too late. She had told me all I wanted to know. She knew what I said. She has something to hide or she would have been delighted to have a chance to air her mother tongue. She lied to me, anyway.'

'Lied?'

'The baker first took three loaves to the door. I counted them as he put them in his basket. That I imagine is the usual order. But it wasn't enough. The baker had to fetch two more. He delivers three times a week. She said there was no one else in the house. Don't ask me to believe that two people, the lady and her husband, eat five loaves in less than two days. Oh no. There's someone else in that house.'

'The missing pilot of the plane?'

'Possibly, but I doubt it.'

'Why are we waiting here?'

'For Diverton. He may tell me the truth. Maybe he won't. If he refuses to talk, our next move will be difficult. We have a tricky problem facing us, and, I'm afraid, a nasty one. I may be wrong, but, although there are still one or two gaps, I believe I have a broad idea of what happened here last night. I'm considering going back to headquarters to report and leave the decision to the Chief.' Biggles smiled faintly.'Alternatively I could pass the buck to the local police and leave them to finish the job.'

'If that's how you feel, old boy, now's your chance. This looks like a police car coming up the lane.'

The car came on, to stop when Biggles raised a hand. In it was a uniformed inspector with a constable at the wheel.

Said Biggles: 'Are you the District Inspector?'

'I am.'

'You're here about the plane crash?'

'That's right. Who are you?'

Biggles produced his identity card. 'I was sent down by my headquarters to look over the machine. There may be a political angle.'

The inspector got out.

Biggles went on: 'The RAF have arrived to dismantle it and take it away, but I've told the officer in charge to

16

leave it alone for the time being. There are one or two things you should see.'

'Couldn't I have found them for myself?'

'You might overlook them. I happen to be an aviation specialist.'

'I see. I heard the plane was a foreigner. You seem to take a serious view of it.'

'I do now.'

The inspector looked dubious. 'Plane crashes are common enough.'

'Not this sort.'

'What's so unusual about it?'

'It wasn't an accident.'

'Oh! Then what was it?'

'Murder – or possibly manslaughter.'

The inspector stared. 'Murder, eh. Are you sure of this?'

'That's how it looks to me.'

'What were you doing when I came along?'

'Waiting for Mr Diverton to come home from market. I'm hoping he'll be able to help us. In fact, I'm sure he could, if he would, but he may be hard to pin down. Do you know him?'

'I've met him once or twice. I believe he's well liked in the district. Takes an interest in the ex-service men's associations, and so on.'

'Do you happen to know if he ever served in the R.A.F?'

'I've never heard that.'

'Never mind. We'll ask him when he comes home.'

'Who's in the house now?'

'Only his wife. So she says. But I have reason to doubt it.'

'Who else could there be?'

'Frankly, I have no idea; but I'd wager there's a man in the house at this moment. At this stage I'd prefer not to guess.'

'Why should Mrs Diverton lie about it?'

'That's what we have to find out.'

'Could it be the pilot of the plane? I hear he hasn't been found.'

'Possibly. But before we go any further please understand that I'm not trying to take this out of your hands. What I suggest is, I'll show you one or two things which, as a pilot myself, I've noticed. Then we'll see Diverton together. Of course, if you'd prefer to act on your own . . .'

'No – no. You're the expert. I'm always willing to take advice from someone who knows his job.'

'Good. I hoped you'd take it like that. We'll have a look at certain evidence that has caught my eye. Then we'll see what explanation Diverton has to offer. You might leave the questions to me in the first instance because they may involve technical aviation.'

'Suits me. As there doesn't appear to be a road to the field I suppose we shall have to leave the car here.'

'I wonder if you'd mind putting it at my disposal for a few minutes? I'd like your driver to run my assistant into Upgates to make some enquiries at the post office which may help to tie things up. It can be done in the time we shall be away.'

'Certainly.'

Biggles turned to Bertie. 'Go to the post office – you may have to find the postman – and ask if any letters bearing foreign stamps have been delivered to Fennels farm recently.'

18

'I'll do that.'

The inspector looked at Biggles curiously but made no comment.

After the car had gone Biggles said: 'This way, Inspector. I'll show you the evidence that supports my theory.'

'What is your theory?'

'You'll grasp it more easily when you've had a look at things.'

They walked briskly to the aircraft. Nothing was said on the way. Reaching it, Biggles said: 'To start with, you can take it from me as an experienced pilot that only one thing could cause a plane, coming in to land, to turn turtle the way this one did; and that was an obstruction fouling the undercarriage, bringing it to a dead stop.'

The inspector looked around. 'I don't see any obstruction.'

'It isn't here now. The man who put it up removed it after it had served its purpose.'

'What was it?'

'I'll show it to you in a moment. Now, if you'll look closely at the undercarriage struts you'll see that both of them, at the same distance from the wheels, have been scratched, scarred, by coming into contact wth something while travelling at speed.'

'I see what you mean,' said the inspector, thoughtfully.

'Now let's go back.'

Just before reaching the gorse bushes Biggles pointed to the hole in the ground. 'Remember that,' he requested. 'There's a similar hole on the far side of the field. There may be others, but I haven't bothered to look for them.' As they went on through the gorse Biggles stopped again and pointed down at some loose turves where the ground had been disturbed. 'If you dig there you might find something interesting,' he remarked, and went on to the barn. He opened the door. 'Make a note of that wire,' he said. 'It could be an important piece of evidence.'

The inspector did not speak, but he looked at his companion with an odd expression.

'I see your car's back,' observed Biggles. 'Let's hear what Sergeant Lissie has to report.'

They joined Bertie, who said: 'You were right. There have been several letters with foreign stamps. Last week there was a telegram.'

'From Spain?'

'Correct. Diverton is here. At least, I assume it was him. He was putting his car in the shed just as we got back.'

'He must have noticed a police car. Did he speak to you?'

'No.'

'All the same, he must be expecting us to call. Let's hear what he has to say. Afterwards, Inspector, as we're on your ground, perhaps you'd like to take over.'

'If that's how you want it.'

'It would be better that way. Let's get on with it. Bertie, you can come.'

'Are you expecting trouble?'

'I think not.'

They went to the door. Biggles knocked. It was opened instantly, as if someone had been watching, by a well-built, keen-eyed, clean-shaven man who was getting on in years. Before anyone else could speak he said in a cultured voice: 'I suppose you're the police making enquiries about the plane that crashed on my land last night.'

'That is correct,' acknowledged Biggles.

'There isn't much I can tell you.'

'On the contrary, I think you may be able to help us quite a lot. May we come in? We won't keep you longer than is necessary.'

'Very well.' Diverton took them into what was obviously the living-room and invited them to be seated. There was no one else there. 'Now, what do you want to know?'

'You say the accident happened last night,' prompted Biggles.

'It must have done.'

'How do you know?'

'Because I walked across the field about eleven o'clock and it wasn't there then.'

'Wasn't that late for you to be out?'

'I'd been to look at a sick ewe.'

'What was the first you knew about it?'

'When a Fleet Air Arm ambulance unit arrived soon after daylight.'

'Did you go to look at the machine?'

'Naturally.'

'What about the pilot?'

'I didn't see him.'

Biggles paused for a moment, his eyes on Diverton's face. 'Tell me, did you by any chance serve in the RFC or RAF during the wars?'

'Yes, I did.'

'Would I be wrong if I guessed you were in the Special Air Service?'

Diverton smiled. 'You'd be right.'

'In which case you'd have a pretty good idea of why the machine in your field crashed.'

Diverton's smile faded. 'No. How would I know?'

'If you served in the SAS you must have heard about fields being trapped to trip up machines putting down spies. It's a fear that hangs over every pilot engaged in special missions. I know. I speak from experience.'

'Now you mention it, I seem to recall something of the sort.'

'The usual trap was a wire stretched tightly across a field. The inevitable result for an aircraft running into it at speed was a somersault.'

'Are you suggesting that's what happened here last night?'

'I'm not suggesting. I'm saying so, definitely. Can you think of anyone who would set such a trap, and why? It must have been someone who knew about the trick.'

Diverton, who had lost some of his confidence, shook his head. 'No,' he said. 'I can't help you there.'

Biggles went on. 'I'm going to ask you some straight questions. You're under no compulsion to answer them, but if you take my advice you will. I shall get the answers sooner or later, if not now. I think I know some of them already, but it would save time if I had your confirmation.'

'I can't imagine why I should be expected to know more than I have already told you,' protested Diverton.

'Let's start from the beginning,' proposed Biggles evenly. 'I believe your wife came originally from Spain?'

'She did. What has that got to do with it?'

'As the plane lying in the field is a Spanish type we

must assume that it came here from Spain. We are bound to associate the two things. I know this could be coincidence, but I have reasons for thinking otherwise. Who else is living in this house apart from you and your wife?'

'My wife's brother is staying with us for a little while.'

'He has been in correspondence with someone in Spain?'

'I didn't say so.'

'I'm saying it.'

'Well, what of it? Is there anything wrong with that?'

'As the result of that correspondence you knew the plane that crashed here was coming. Am I right?'

No answer.

'The possibility of it landing here gave you cause for anxiety, if not alarm? Correct me if I'm wrong.'

No answer.

'You decided to take steps to prevent a normal landing.'

Still Diverton did not speak. Biggles' face seemed to fascinate him.

'Which of you set the trap? You or your brother-in-law?'

Diverton moistened his lips. His face was pale.

'As you would know about such anti-aircraft methods I must conclude that the idea, at least, was yours,' pursued Biggles relentlessly. 'Oh, come on, Diverton, out with it. I've seen the abrasions on the undercarriage struts. I've seen the stake holes. The wire is in your barn. Why not tell us the whole truth? As a pilot yourself I'm sure you wouldn't deliberately crash an aircraft without a good reason. Why did you do it? Would you rather we dug up what you buried in the gorse bushes? Was it the body of the pilot?

Diverton nodded. Trembling, he said bitterly: 'You're too clever. I should have known. With only the accident people to deal with I was hoping to get away with it. I didn't reckon on an old hand like you coming along to investigate. All right. I'll tell you everything. Then I hope you'll understand. A man must stand by his relatives when they're in trouble – above all, his wife.'

'With that I agree – up to a point.'

'The explanation of the whole thing is really quite simple,' went on Diverton. 'My brother-in-law came here as a political refugee from the present régime in Spain.'

'Was his offence criminal?' interposed Biggles sharply.

'No. Nothing like that. Purely political. He, with others, plotted to overthrow the government. Neither my wife nor I knew anything about this at the time. The plot was betrayed. Most of the conspirators were caught and shot. Carlos, my wife's brother, was one of the few who got away. He found safety here, temporarily, at all events. But they were determined to get him. You know how it is with dictators. Fortunately Carlos still had friends in Spain, some in high places. Through them he was kept informed of what was happening. Through them we learned that government agents had discovered Carlos was living here with his sister. Carlos was not only my wife's brother; he was also a close friend of mine. In those circumstances I couldn't refuse him hospitality, even though I didn't agree with his politics.'

'I understand that,' put in Biggles.

'The next step was inevitable. We heard, through the

same source of information, that an agent had been detailed to kill Carlos before he could apply for political asylum in this country, as was his intention. That would have made him more difficult to get at, so it was decided to liquidate him right away. We were told this property had been photographed from the air, so the plan was fairly obvious. My big field was a ready-made landing ground. It would be easy for the killer to fly over at night, land, do his dirty work and return home without anyone being aware of his visit. By planting a bomb in or near the house he might have killed all three of us. We had to take precautions.'

'That sounds plausible,' conceded Biggles. 'Go on.'

'The trouble was we didn't know when this man would come. It might be any time. It wasn't practicable to sit up night after night waiting for him, so as a result of my war-time experience I used the old trick of preventing a plane from landing clandestinely. I rigged up the wire at sundown and took it up at dawn.' Diverton smiled wanly. 'I didn't want to trap one of our own machines making a forced landing. Well, it worked. The agent came and ran into the trap. That's all.'

'Not quite all. What happened to him?'

'He was killed landing. His neck was broken, presumably by the sudden jolt. I ask you to believe me when I say I didn't reckon on that.'

Biggles nodded. 'I've heard of that happening.'

'Actually, I was awake and heard the plane coming,' resumed Diverton. 'I heard the crash. It was in the early hours. I got up and went out. Carlos came with me. Finding the pilot dead put us in a flap, as you can imagine. We didn't want questions asked, so after some

25

discussion we decided to bury him and say nothing. I'm not going to pretend I shed any tears. He came to commit cold-blooded murder.'

'You buried him in the gorse?'

'Yes.'

'Did you hope to get away with that? The pilot of a foreign plane had to be accounted for.'

'It may sound stupid to you, but it seemed reasonable to us at the time. Our intention was, having buried the body, as soon as it was daylight to set fire to the machine and so destroy all signs of its identity. The crash could have remained a mystery. We dared not start the fire at night because it would be seen from a long way off. We were out of luck. At the crack of dawn what should fly over, low, but a Fleet Air Arm chopper. We knew the pilot had spotted the crash because he circled over it. As he must have seen the Spanish identification markings there was no point after that in burning the machine. All we could do was take everything out of the cockpit, maps, photographs, navigation notes, etc., and do away with them. That's the truth, and the whole truth. Right or wrong. I still believe that if that damned helicopter hadn't come over we might have got away with it.'

Biggles agreed.

'Is there anything else you want to know?' asked Diverton. 'I'm in your hands. All I ask is, don't send Carlos back to Spain, because if you do it will mean certain death for him. He'll confirm what I've said. Do you want to see him?'

'I don't think so.' Biggles looked at the inspector. 'Have you any questions?'

'Not now.'

'Then it's all yours. I'll leave the rest to you.'

'I suppose I'm under arrest,' said the ex-pilot wearily.

The inspector looked uncertain. 'I shall have to take instructions on that. If you'll give me your word that none of you in this house will leave the farm until you hear from me again you can stay here and look after your sheep.'

'You have my oath on that,' said Diverton, readily. 'I've nowhere else to go. Everything I possess is tied up here.'

'All right,' concluded the inspector. 'We'll leave it like that for the time being.'

Biggles got up. 'Come on, Bertie. Let's go home.'

After some delay, in which more than one British government department had to be consulted, no action was taken against Diverton, his wife, or brother-in-law who, in the meantime, had applied for political asylum in Britain. In fact, it might almost be said that the case was hushed up when it was realised that to bring the matter into open court could have repercussions better avoided. There was never any question of murder. Diverton was able to produce letters which showed that the only deliberate murder intended was on the part of the foreign pilot who came at night for that purpose. A charge of manslaughter was considered, but even this was ruled out on the grounds that what Diverton had done was justifiable self-protection.

With which decision Biggles was in full agreement.

Chapter 2

A RING O' ROSES

On a periodical tour of some of the smaller flying establishments Biggles was in Essex, in the club-house of Icarus Aviation, having a drink at the bar with Clinton, secretary and senior instructor, when to the delight of the pupils present an aircraft made a spectacular 'falling-leaf' landing and taxied on to the sheds.

'Do you encourage that sort of show-off over the aerodrome?' he enquired.

Clinton shrugged a shoulder.

'What is that racy-looking job? I don't seem to know it,' went on Biggles.

'A new French product,' explained Clinton. 'They call it the *Coursier*. Only one or two have been built so far. I don't think they'll sell it over here.'

'Why not?'

'It's too expensive, both to buy and to run.'

'Does it belong to one of your members?'

'Yes. Nice lad. He'll be along presently after putting his machine in its hangar. He insists on doing that himself. He's a Persian* named Zand. Kerman Zand. He claims to be of the old Persian nobility. Oodles of money. Here he comes now.'

The new arrival was greeted in a manner that proclaimed popularity. He was a slightly built young

*The country of Persia is now known as Iran.

man, dark-skinned, with finely cut features, teeth like pearls, and sparkling black eyes. With a smile and effusive gestures he ordered drinks all round – which may have accounted for his popularity.

'What's he doing over here?' asked Biggles.

'His old man's in business, very exclusive, which means pricey. Cosmetics. He runs it from one of those big old Georgian houses, Zand House, near Regent's Park. Zand Cosmetics Ltd. You sometimes see their advertisements in the glossy magazines. They have branches on the Continent. You must have heard of a perfume called "Rosa Luna". The trade mark of Zand Cosmetics is a Persian dancing girl wearing a *yashmak* – and not much else.'

'I haven't noticed it.'

' "Rosa Luna", in other words Rose of the Moon, is like no other perfume on earth. That's why it commands the price it does. Kerman acts as his father's overseas agent. He's just back from abroad now.' Clinton grinned. 'He's a walking advertisement for the family product, as you won't fail to notice if he comes near you. He puts it in his hair-oil.'

The subject of the conversation, a bottle of champagne in one hand and a glass in the other, joined them. He also brought with him a strong waft of perfume which, while wonderfully fragrant, produced a faint frown of disapproval in Biggles' eyes.

'Not drinking?' questioned the Persian, reprovingly, looking at Biggles' empty glass. His English was fluent, with the merest trace of accent.

'I've just had one, thanks,' declined Biggles.

'Have another.'

'Not now. One's my limit when I'm flying.'

'Be careful,' Clinton said, in an affected confidential voice. 'He's a cop.'

The Persian's eyes opened wide. 'Really! What fun. How's business?'

'Not too bad.'

'Caught any naughty boys lately?'

'We pick up one here and there, once in a while.'

'From what I read in the papers, no matter how smart the cops are the crooks are always one jump ahead.'

'That's because the crooks get the publicity,' returned Biggles evenly. 'You only hear of the police when they *fail* to get their man.'

'Seems a bit hard.'

'It suits us. We prefer to keep out of the limelight. Had a good trip?'

'Very good.'

'Been far?'

'Only to Paris.' Zand looked at the clock. 'Sorry to rush away, but I must be getting home. My people get worried if I'm late.' To Clinton he went on: 'I shan't be wanting the machine again until next week. I've put the papers in your office. You haven't sent me a bill yet for the new tank. Let me have it and I'll send you a cheque. Cheerio.' With boisterous farewells the Persian departed.

'I take it he has a car,' said Biggles.

'Yes. He's just bought a new Jaguar. There it is. He leaves it here when he's away on one of his trips.'

'What did he mean about a new tank?'

'He got us to fit an emergency tank in the *Coursier*. Quite small. Only five gallons.'

'Does he have far to go then?'

'I don't think he goes beyond the firm's continental branches.'

'Does he do any flying here?'

'Practically none. He learnt to fly here about two years ago. He's a born pilot.'

'Where are these overseas branches?'

Clinton gave Biggles a questioning look. 'Why do you want to know?'

'Just for the record. I like to know where privately owned machines go when they cross the Channel regularly.'

'You surely don't suspect him of any funny business? You can take it from me he's all right.'

Biggles shrugged. 'It could be in his own interest that we should know where he goes. If one day he had a crack-up we should know where to look for him. How often does he go abroad?'

'Practically every weekend. Goes on Sunday and comes back Monday morning. Come to the office. He writes on the firm's notepaper. The names of the branches are on it.'

They went to the office. Clinton took a letter from a tray. 'Here you are. London, Paris, Brussels, Geneva and Milan. Anything else you want to know?' he asked with a hint of sarcasm.

Biggles ignored it. 'Are those the papers he mentioned?' He indicated a wallet lying on the desk.

'Probably. Do you want to look at 'em?'

'You might check where he landed in France and where he cleared Customs on his return.'

Clinton frowned. 'My God! You are a nosy-parker.'

'I'm a copper – remember? On my job suspicion becomes second nature.'

Clinton unfolded the documents. 'Here you are. Paris, Le Bourget. That was yesterday. Southend, stamped this morning. All in order. Now I hope you're satisfied.'

Biggles nodded. 'Good enough. I'll be getting along. Don't forget, Clinton, people are not always what they appear to be. I have to ferret out those who aren't. That's not only in the public interest, it's in yours. Better not tell Zand I was interested in his business – it might upset him. Be seeing you again sometime.' He went out, got into his Auster and took off.

As soon as he was in the air he called the Air Police Operations office on its own radio wavelength. When Ginger answered he said: 'This is urgent. Go to Zand House, Regent's Park, and watch for a dark green Jag. to stop there. Check if anything is taken into the house from the car. Is that clear? Over.'

'Roger. Over.'

'That's all. See you presently.'

An hour later Biggles walked into the office to find Ginger there. 'Well?' he queried.

Ginger answered. 'The car came. One man in it. Foreign-looking type. He took into the house, first, from the boot, a couple of two-gallon petrol cans. He then fetched a small suitcase from the front seat. That's all.'

'Somewhere in the files there should be specification and performance figures, English version, of a new French light plane called the *Coursier*. Look it up. I want to know the endurance range.'

'Here we are. Eight hundred miles. Anything else?'

'The man who got out of the car was a Persian named Kerman Zand. Apparently he holds a pilot's ticket. Check that it's in order.'

Ginger did so. 'Okay,' he reported. 'No trouble. Anything else?'

'Not now.'

Ginger closed the filing cabinet. 'What goes on?'

Biggles narrated what had happened at the Icarus Aviation airfield. 'There may be nothing in it, but . . . I wouldn't trust that young man the length of Whitehall. He chucks money about too freely. I know that's only intuition – or, if you like, experience; but there's more than that. He's had an extra fuel tank fitted. Why does he want that if, as he says, he only goes abroad to visit the firm's branches on the Continent, all of which are well within the range of the standard version of *Coursier*? He goes on Sunday and returns on Monday morning. What does he do? As people don't normally work on Sunday one would expect the offices to be closed.'

'It doesn't quite add up,' conceded Ginger.

'I'll tell you something else. When Clinton told him jokingly I was a copper, just for a split second a look, a sort of hooded look, came into his eyes. His lips were still smiling. He could control his expression but not what was in his brain. The tip of his nose went white. That's always a sign of anxiety. A man can't prevent that, either. A judge once told me it's an almost certain way to tell if a witness is lying. The moment he departs from the truth he gets an anxiety complex, a natural reaction from fear he may be caught out. That's all. Knowing that trivial things can sometimes tot up to make a big one, I'm bound to wonder what this young man is up to.'

'The answer might be in those petrol cans. What could it be?'

'I'm pretty sure it wasn't petrol. There's nothing odd

about having a spare can of petrol in your car; but when you get home you don't take it into the house.'

'Could it be perfume? There's a heavy duty on it.'

'Possibly, but I would hardly think so. Much of the money saved in tax would be lost in the cost of air transportation. Yet for a small firm this one seems to be making a great deal of money. How is it done?'

'You say they're Persians. Could it be anything to do with Persia? What does Persia produce?'

'A good many things. Oil, of course, and carpets; all sorts of metals, including a certain amount of gold and silver. Some good turquoise; I can't remember everything. I believe they produce some opium . . .'

'Could drugs be the answer?'

'I doubt it. If the Zands wanted opium no doubt they could get it without bringing it from Persia. No. If something irregular is going on one would expect it to be something to do with their business, which is cosmetics. Apparently their sales have been pushed up by a very exclusive perfume called "Rosa Luna", of which they hold the secret. Young Zand reeked of it. Clinton says it's in the hair-oil he uses. But this guessing is getting us nowhere. All we can do is watch this young man. It won't be easy, because I could see Clinton resented me asking questions. Zand is the blue-eyed boy at Garfold – that's the name of the airfield – largely, I suspect, because he treats champagne like soda-water.'

'Why not take the bull by the horns and warn the Customs people at Southend that you're suspicious? They're experts. If Zand is carrying contraband they'll find it.'

'Yes, and if they drew blank we'd look silly.'

'Then catch him when he parks his machine at Garfold. That's where he must put the stuff in his car to take it home.'

'That gives me an idea. Have you ever been to Garfold?'

'Never.'

'So Clinton doesn't know you?'

'I don't know anyone there.'

'Good. Early next Monday morning you'll fly down. Pretend you're a pupil from another club doing a cross-country. You're having trouble. Engine cutting out and picking up again. You don't think the machine's safe to fly as it is. Can they do something about it? While they're working on it you'll be able to wander about. If the Jaguar is there, and the *Coursier* isn't in the hangar, you'll know Zand is in the air. When he comes in and puts his machine in the hangar, without letting him see you, watch exactly what he does. Get the idea?'

Smiling, Ginger nodded.

'Fine. Let's leave it at that.'

The following Monday at noon Ginger walked into the Operations Room carrying flying cap and goggles.

Biggles was waiting. 'Well, how did you get on?'

'He's up to something. I'll tell you what happened. The plan about me having engine trouble worked. The *Coursier* was away. At eleven o'clock it rolled up. I went into the hangar and watched from the tool room. Zand taxied in and got out. He was wearing a leather jacket with a fur collar. He took off his jacket and after a quick look round unzipped what must have been a little pocket in the fur collar. He took out six small objects, made of glass, I think, and put them carefully in a

35

waistcoat pocket, each one wrapped in cotton wool. That's how I was able to count them. This took less than a minute. After another look round he fetched two empty petrol cans from several piled in a corner and filled them from his auxiliary tank. He carried these to his car and went on to the club-house. I went back to the hangar and had a sniff at the spare tank.'

'Perfume.'

'No. And it wasn't petrol. But the smell had a volatile quality as if it was some sort of spirit.'

'Not brandy, whisky . . . ?'

'No, nothing like that. As that was all I could do and they'd told me they could find nothing wrong with my aircraft I came home.'

'Good work. At least we know he's carrying something illicit or it wouldn't be necessary for him to have a secret pocket in his flying jacket. We shall only find out what it is by catching him with the stuff in his hand. To do that means we shall have to wait until next Monday. We'll go down together and risk a show-down. If he's innocent, and the decent chap everyone seems to think he is, he won't complain. If he isn't – well, he won't be able to. It begins to look as if this bright young man is making the oldest mistake in crime. Having pulled off something once, he imagines he can get away with it for ever. The cocky little rascal had the impudence to sneer at me that the police were always one jump behind the crooks. It's time he was cut down to size. It'd be a pleasure to clip his wings.'

Another week passed. Ten-thirty on Monday morning saw the police Auster on Garfold airfield parked near the hangars. 'There's the Jaguar, but I don't see the *Coursier*,' remarked Biggles to Ginger as they got out.

'Are you going to wait in the club-house?'

'No. I'd rather not see Clinton. He might try to interfere. We'll go behind the hangars. We shall see the *Coursier* when it comes in.'

This they did. Time passed. A little before eleven the *Coursier* appeared. At the same time Clinton came round the end hangar looking anything but friendly.

'I saw your machine,' he said shortly.' What do you think you're doing?'

'I haven't time to tell you now,' answered Biggles, in the same tone of voice. 'Go to your office and stay there.'

Clinton stared. 'Are you telling me . . . ?'

Biggles cut in succinctly. 'Listen, Clinton. If you don't do as I tell you, you may find yourself in trouble for obstructing the police. That could cost you your licence.'

Clinton's jaw sagged. 'If you think Zand . . .'

'Go to your office and stay there. Don't speak to anyone on the way.'

The pilot turned and strode off.

Biggles and Ginger hurried into Zand's hangar and took up position in the tool room which had a window looking into the main body of the hangar.

Presently the *Coursier* taxied in. The ignition was cut. The airscrew died. The sole occupant, Zand, got down. With his back to the watchers he took off his jacket, felt round the collar and pulled a zip fastener. The sound could be heard distinctly.

Biggles walked up quietly behind him. He said: 'I think you know me. I'm a police officer. May I see what you have there?'

Zand spun round in such haste that a tiny object fell to the concrete floor. It broke. A dark, turgid liquid

37

oozed out. 'You interfering fool,' he rasped. 'Look what you've done.'

'You're not compelled to answer my questions, but I would advise you to do so,' returned Biggles, without raising his voice. 'What is it?'

'Find out.'

'You can rely on me to do that.' Stooping, Biggles touched the liquid with a finger and raised it to his nose. He grimaced. 'I also intend to examine the contents of your extra tank,' he stated.

The next moment he came near to losing his life.

Showing his teeth like an animal, spitting out: 'You cunning swine,' Zand leapt at him with a dagger upraised.

Biggles jumped sideways. The dagger gashed the shoulder of his jacket. It was as close as that. Ginger put out a foot. Zand, carried forward by his lunge, tripped over it and fell. Before he could get up Ginger was kneeling on his back, with Biggles holding down the hand that held the weapon. He twisted it viciously. Zand cried out in pain. The dagger fell clear. Biggles tossed it aside. 'This won't improve matters for you,' he snapped through his teeth. 'Now behave yourself, you murdering little devil, or I'll give you what you deserve right here and now.'

A voice spoke. 'What's going on here?' Clinton strode up, his face livid.

'I told you to stay in your office, but since you prefer to be involved in criminal proceedings you can make yourself useful,' Biggles told him sternly. 'Go and phone for a police car. I suspected this young man of smuggling. He's just tried to murder me.'

'I'm sorry if . . .'

'Don't waste time apologising. Get on with it.'

Clinton hurried off.

Biggles took possession of several small glass phials, as the objects turned out to be, which he found in the fur collar.

Zand, shaking, his face grey, was allowed to get up. 'I – I lost my temper,' he stammered. 'I'm sorry.'

'You will be,' Biggles told him grimly. 'Now, what is this stuff?'

Zand ran his tongue over his lips. 'I suppose you'll find out,' he muttered. 'Attar of roses. The real thing. Special Persian roses. It's the base of our perfume "Rosa Luna". In that broken phial was the essence of a million roses.' The Persian seemed to be on the point of tears.

'Why didn't you declare it?'

'Each of those phials is worth nearly two hundred pounds. The duty would have been too heavy.'

'And what is in that tank?'

'Absolute alcohol. You can only get it as rectified as that at one place in France.'

Biggles looked curious. 'How much attar of roses do you put in a gallon of spirit to make your perfume?'

'A few drops only.'

'What do you charge for the stuff?'

'Twenty pounds an ounce bottle.'

'And you've just brought in four gallons of spirit. At twenty fluid ounces to a pint, if my arithmetic is any good that would have made twelve thousand pounds' worth of perfume.'

'About that.'

Biggles shook his head. 'No wonder you can afford to buy expensive aeroplanes and motor-cars.'

Clinton came in. 'The police car is here,' he said.

The firm of Zand Cosmetics Ltd no longer exists. The directors are in prison.

Talking over the case afterwards, with an encyclopedia open in front of him Ginger said: 'When we were discussing Persian products we missed one important item. Listen to this.' He read: ' "Attar of roses. The essence of *Rosa centifolia* or *Rosa damascena*, produced by distillation in water, the oil then being collected from the surface by means of a feather. It is chiefly prepared in Persia and Turkey, from which countries it is exported in small phials. It is very costly and is in itself too strong to be pleasant, but a few drops of it will scent a great quantity of spirit." '

'Which all goes to show that today a copper is expected to know everything,' murmured Biggles sadly.

Returned Ginger, grinning. 'It looks as if we shall have to carry an encyclopedia around with us.'

Biggles shook his head. 'Not me. You know what they say. You can't teach an old dog new tricks.'

Chapter 3

THE LONG CHASE

From five thousand feet, under a sky almost clear of cloud, the streams of traffic on the Great North Road looked like colonies of ants on the march, one heading north, the other south.

Biggles, testing new long-range two-way radio equipment which had just been installed in the Air Police Auster 'Autocrat', paying no attention to what was going on below, continued a widening circle over outer London, checking all points of the compass for possible interference. From time to time he glanced at Bertie who, wearing earphones, occupied the seat beside him.

'How's it going?'

'Top-hole. Clear as a bell. I've just been listening to Ginger, speaking from Gaskin's office. He's been giving me a running commentary on a big wages snatch outside a bank in Hampstead.'

'How's he doing that? If he's in Gaskin's office what does he know about it?'

'Gaskin is hot on the trail of the bandits in a radio car. They got away with the swag in a red sports car and he's keeping the Yard informed of the route they're taking, hoping road blocks will stop 'em.'

Biggles looked interested. 'Where are the bandits now?'

'They're just through Hatfield.'

'Heading north?'

'Yes.'

'With Gaskin still after them?'

'Yes.'

'How far is he behind them?'

'Can't be far. He catches a glimpse of 'em from time to time; but as they're ignoring traffic lights he hasn't been able to overtake them. They've already caused two accidents. They've been travelling faster than road blocks can be set up.'

'What else has Ginger told you? How many bandits were there?'

'Two.'

'Could they be identified?'

'No. They wore stockings over their faces. They can afford to take risks, knowing they'll be for the high jump if they're caught. They shot and killed a policeman who saw the raid and tried to stop 'em.'

'The devils! We may be able to do something to help. A sports car being chased by a police car shouldn't be hard to spot. Keep in touch with Ginger for the latest news. Tell him what we're doing. Ask him to relay everything Gaskin says.'

Bertie complied.

Already the Auster had its nose down for speed and in a minute Hatfield was in sight, with the broad grey ribbon of the Great North Road running on beyond. Biggles did not speak. His eyes were exploring the north-bound traffic for a red sports car, travelling at racing speed, with a black police car in pursuit.

The Auster was down to two thousand when Bertie said: 'They've turned off the main road at Baldock. Now heading east on the A505 for Royston.'

'Ah! That's to dodge the road blocks.'

'I suppose so.'

This was followed by a rather long silence. Then Bertie burst out: 'Gaskin's lost 'em.'

'*What!* How?'

'They're away in a plane.'

'A *plane*. How the devil . . . ?'

'Just a minute. Ginger's coming in again . . . Gaskin says they must have known the plane was there – waiting for 'em – part of the getaway plan. He found the red car – a stolen Jag. – up a lane. He overshot it before he spotted it. By the time he could stop, two men with a suitcase were running across a field. A plane was there with its engine running. Before Gaskin could do anything they were away. There was nothing he could do – except swear.'

'Did he recognise the type of plane?'

'No. All he can say is it was a monoplane.'

'That's a fat lot of good. Did he get its registration letters?'

'No. It took off directly away from him. All he can say is it was a small plane painted white or silver. A light colour, anyway. He watched it out of sight. It was flying north when it disappeared.'

'If the plane was there waiting it must have had a pilot. That makes three of 'em; so the plane must have been at least a three-seater. If it stays on a northerly track we may be able to spot it. They won't expect an aircraft to trail them, so it's likely they'll travel at cruising speed. If so we should be able to catch 'em.'

The police Auster was now racing north on full throttle with Biggles' eyes probing the sky ahead. It was a typical spring day, mostly clear but with occasional fronts of high, fleecy, cumulus clouds. Some were showing above the northern horizon.

Apparently Bertie noticed them, for he remarked: 'If they get into that stuff we shan't have much hope of finding them.'

'Not imagining they're being followed it's likely they'll keep out of it. A pilot doesn't fly blind from choice. Tell Ginger what we're doing and ask for a met. report on the weather further north. Urgent.'

While Bertie was waiting for this information to come through the Auster was kicking the air behind it at top speed, with Biggles' eyes scrutinising the sky ahead, section by section, with the methodical thoroughness that comes from war experience.

'Light broken cloud, sky six tenths covered nearing the Border: increasing overcast further north,' reported Bertie.

'If only I can spot that machine before we get as far north as that I'll see it doesn't lose me,' muttered Biggles. 'Has Ginger any more news?'

'No, Gaskin is coming home. Now we're on the trail he'll stand by.'

'Good thing we were topped up when we started. We shan't have to worry about petrol.'

'Suppose the plane goes abroad?'

'Why should it be flying north if it intended to do that? But the first thing is to find it. Hold hard! I may have got it. I can see a machine against that cloud dead ahead.'

Bertie stared. 'You're right, old boy. Little feller, too. How are we going to know if it's the one we're after?'

'We shan't know till it touches down somewhere. I shall be with it. The one we want will have the money on board.'

44

'You're not forgetting these johnnies have guns. They've already shot one copper so they've nothing to lose by shooting another.'

'We'll deal with that situation should it arise,' answered Biggles grimly, his eyes still on the speck ahead, clear against a white background of cloud and travelling directly away from them. 'We should be able to catch up on him. As long as he doesn't realise he's being tracked he'll probably be content to carry on at cruising speed. I'll get a bit closer – but not too close.'

'They're climbing. They must have decided to go over that next cloud formation.'

'So would I were I in their shoes – assuming they're the men we want. They wouldn't overlook the possibility of people on the ground being alerted to watch for them. They'll keep out of sight if they can.'

'They might take to the clouds. Then what?'

Biggles smiled faintly. 'I've played this game before. I'll see they don't lose me. Tell Ginger we may have sighted the bandits. We'll give him our position from time to time. Gaskin can make what use of it he likes.'

The chase continued. Nothing more was said for a time. Then Bertie, still in touch with Ginger, reported: 'Gaskin is back at the Yard. He's raging at having lost his men. He says if we tell him where the plane lands he'll come along.'

'What's he talking about? If we keep on as we're going we shall soon be in Scotland, so if he wants to be in at the death he'll have a devil of a long way to come.'

Presently Biggles continued. 'By thunder! I believe we *are* going to Scotland. East Scotland. I'll tell you something. The pilot in front of us is following the A.1.'

'Why East Scotland?'

'From the way he jinked when he was in the clear over Scotch Corner. The road forks there. Had he been going to West Scotland he would have taken the left fork. He took the right. That's Darlington below. I'd say the man at the stick knows the way north by road, but I doubt if he's flown over it before. He's not using his compass. He's flying with his eyes on the ground.'

Durham and Newcastle slid away below. 'It looks as if I was right,' resumed Biggles. 'There's Alnwick ahead. We shall soon be over the Border. Had he been going down short of it he'd have started losing some altitude. Are you still in touch with Ginger?'

'Yes.'

'Tell him where we are.'

Having done so, Bertie turned to Biggles. 'Shall I tell you what I think?'

'I'm listening.'

'The chap in front has spotted us in his reflector. He's realised we're following him and is trying to run us out of petrol.'

'Could be. But if that's his idea he's on a loser. Unless that machine has some extra long-range tankage he'll be out of juice before we are. There is this about it. He isn't going overseas. If, as I believe, the machine is an Auster, he can't have enough petrol left to reach Ireland or the Continent. With our extra tank we should be able to outfly him. We'll get him at the end.'

The chase continued for some time without any serious change in the weather conditions, although after crossing the Firth of Forth the meteorological office proved to be right in the matter of increasing cloud. Great 'cauliflowers' of cumulus were rolling in from the north-west to more than half cover the ground.

For a while the fugitive pilot went round them, but as they thickened he went above them. After leaving Perth astern he went down again; but he still showed no sign of landing.

'I fancy he's not sure of his position,' said Biggles, closing the gap between them. 'Where the devil can he be going? I wasn't prepared for a trip like this.'

'I tell you, he knows we're after him and isn't going down until he's shaken us off his tail.'

'I'm beginning to think you're right. Well, he can't go much further. Neither can we if it comes to that. Look where we are. Those are the Cairngorms in front. He can't get down there, that's certain. If he tries it he's liable to find the clouds have rocks in 'em.'

Both machines were now at about five thousand feet over the rugged peaks of the Cairngorm massif, still showing snow on the high tops and north-facing slopes, when Bertie remarked: 'We look like losing this bird after all. 'That's a solid-looking layer of overcast ahead of us. Sky must be pretty well covered. We can't follow him in that lot.'

'It depends on whether he stays above or goes below.'

'If he holds his height he'll be above.'

'Sooner or later he'll have to go through to see where he is. He must have known where he was going and prepared for it, or he'd have been out of petrol before this, even though the pilot filled his tanks somewhere down south in readiness for the getaway.' Biggles glanced at his petrol gauge. 'If this goes on much longer we shall end up ourselves by looking for somewhere to get our wheels on the carpet. Where the devil can the man be making for?'

'Lossiemouth?'

'A Fleet Air Arm station? I can't see him landing there with or without a load of stolen money on board. We're north of Aberdeen. He might try Dalcross, although at the moment he isn't on a course for Inverness. Are you still in contact with Ginger?'

'Yes, but at this distance there's some interference. Gaskin is still with him.'

'Give him our position. All I can say is I think we're somewhere over Morayshire.'

'He wants to know the type of machine we're after.'

'We're still not sure. We've only seen it end on from behind. It may be an Auster.'

Another pause. Then Bertie said: 'Ginger says Gaskin is talking of coming up.'

'What does he think he's going to do? It'll be dark in an hour.'

'He's mad to get his hands on the crook who shot the policeman. He reckons we shan't get back tonight whatever happens. Where are we most likely to refuel?'

'Probably Dalcross. I know of nowhere else within reach. In that case, if we sleep anywhere, it will be in Inverness. Station Hotel. We've stayed there before, so they know us.'

While Bertie was passing on this information, both aircraft, under a darkening sky, had reached the overcast. It appeared to be unbroken.

'I must say I don't care much for this,' said Bertie, frowning. 'From what I know of the country under this murk it's no place to run out of petrol.'

'The fellow in front must be raving mad – unless he knows of a private airfield handy,' growled Biggles.

'Watch out! There he goes.'

A gap, little more than a hole, like a tear in a blanket,

had appeared in the cloud-layer, and the leading machine was diving for it at a steep angle. Biggles, who had closed the distance between them to a few hundred yards, also made a rush for it; but before he had reached the spot the banks of vapour, gold-tinted where they caught the rays of the setting sun, had rolled together, sealing the opening.

Said Bertie, lugubriously: 'He knows he's being shadowed. He's fooled us.'

'Not yet,' snapped Biggles, as another hole appeared, only to start closing again. He stood the Auster on its nose and went down like a stooping falcon. The hole closed behind him as he went through it. 'Look for him,' he rapped out. 'He can't be far away.'

Under the far-reaching overcast, the ground, about a thousand feet below it, lay dull and gloomy in a dismal twilight, a wide expanse of moor, apparently heather, since there were only occasional areas of cultivation. Across it a single narrow road lay like a carelessly dropped piece of tape. Horizons faded into a colourless blur. At widely spaced intervals black patches of curiously geometrical patterns marked what were obviously Forestry Commission plantations.

'I've got him,' said Bertie sharply. 'There he goes, skimming that long stand of timber half left, near the road.'

'By gosh! He's low. He can't be going to land there. What the devil does he think he's doing?'

'Trying to give us the slip.'

'Pin-point the spot on the map. Of course, if these plantations are recent they won't be marked on it. Note those two small pools on the other side of the road.'

'He's climbing again,' observed Bertie.

'He's changed course, too. Due north. We must be near the sea. There it is.'

'Must be the Moray Firth. Can his objective be Invergordon?'

'If it is we've been following the wrong machine. What's that town ahead?'

'Nairn – or maybe Forres. Wouldn't swear to either. It . . .'

'He's going down,' broke in Biggles. 'This must be it. Tell Ginger.'

'I've never heard of an aerodrome here.'

'Nor I. But I can see a big field with a windsock. There's a building of some sort to one side. Must be a private airstrip. Watch him.'

The leading aircraft had lined up with the big field with the obvious intention of going down.

'What are we going to do?' asked Bertie.

'Follow him in.'

'We shall look a pair of twits if we've chased an innocent aircraft five hundred miles.'

'I wouldn't see anything funny in that. We shall know more about it when we've searched that plane.'

'They may object.'

'Not if they have nothing to hide. Keep your eyes on that machine while I'm getting down. Check the number of people who get out and if they carry any luggage. I see it *is* an Auster. Take its registration.'

The plane which had been followed for so long now glided in, and having touched down ran on to stop near a dilapidated-looking cottage.

'Three men getting out,' reported Bertie, while Biggles was occupied with landing. 'They've gone to the house. Now standing watching us.'

'Any luggage?'

'Nothing.'

Having landed, Biggles taxied on to the other machine. Its colour was not exactly white, or grey, but more of a biscuit tint. To Bertie he said shortly, as he switched off: 'I'm going to search that machine. The stolen money was in a suitcase. Whatever it's in now must make a fair-sized parcel, so it can't be overlooked. There may be trouble. If there is it should be enough to tell us all we want to know. Honest men would co-operate. I haven't come all this way to be put off by some footling argument.'

Biggles got down and with Bertie in attendance advanced to the three men who, with drinks in their hands, stood waiting at the door of the cottage. One was young, in his early twenties, and, wearing an RAF tie, presumably the pilot. The other two were of an entirely different type, middle-aged and thickset, with hard expressions and calculating eyes.

Said the pilot, jokingly: 'Are you the chaps who have been on my tail all the way from England?'

'That's right.'

'What's the idea?'

Biggles answered the question with another. Looking around he enquired: 'What is this place?'

'North-East Highlands Flying Club.'

'It doesn't look much like a flying club to me.'

'We've only been functioning for a couple of weeks. We're not properly organised yet.'

'I don't remember you applying for a licence to operate.'

One of the other men spoke. 'What do you mean – *you* don't remember. What's it got to do with you? Who are

51

you, anyhow?'

'We're air police officers. Here's my card, if you want to see it.'

The pilot came in again. 'How interesting. What are you hoping to find here?'

Again Biggles ignored the question. 'You won't mind if we look over your machine?'

The pilot grinned. 'Go right ahead.'

Biggles did not smile. With an inclination of his head he said to Bertie: 'Take a look.'

Bertie went off. No objection was raised. Said the pilot: 'Care for a drink?'

'No thanks.'

'What's all this nonsense about a licence?'

'As a pilot you should know.'

'I haven't long been out of the Air Force.'

'Then you'd better make yourself acquainted with Civil Flying Regulations. What's your name?'

'Duncan. Murdo Duncan. Ex-Flying Officer, RAF.'

'You come from these parts?'

'Inverness.'

Bertie came back. 'Nothing,' he said quietly.

Biggles did not show any chagrin he may have felt. 'Sorry you've been troubled,' he said evenly.

Said the pilot: 'Just as a matter of curiosity, what were you looking for?'

'A serious crime was committed in London earlier in the day and the crooks got away in an aircraft.'

'How much money was stolen?'

'I didn't say anything about money. A police officer was murdered. We're looking for the thug who killed him.' Biggles spoke with his eyes on the pilot's face.

There was a brief silence. Then, after a glance at the

darkening sky, Biggles went on: 'Well, we'll be getting along.'

'Where are you going now?' asked Duncan.

'Probably Dalcross. I need petrol. Don't forget what I said about regulations.' Biggles turned away.

Not until they were in the machine, and airborne, did Bertie speak. 'What a sell-out,' he sighed.

'Don't jump to conclusions.'

'Aren't you satisfied. . . ?'

'I'd make a wager that was the getaway plane.'

'But there's nothing in it. I went over it from prop boss to tail skid.'

'I'll take your word for it. There's nothing in it *now*.'

'They didn't unload anything. I never took my eyes off them. Why are you still suspicious?'

'I could give you several reasons. Did you happen to be looking at the pilot's face when I said a policeman had been murdered?'

'No.'

'If you had you'd have seen him change colour. That's something a guilty man can't prevent. I'd say he was prepared for robbery, but not for murder. He's probably new to crime. I could have asked a lot more questions: why had they been to England: who owned the aircraft: who were the passengers, and so on, but I decided it was better to let them think they'd fooled us. We haven't finished yet. Let's get to Dalcross for a start. We haven't far to go. Then we'll find quarters in Inverness. It's time we had something to eat.'

It was nearly nine o'clock when Biggles, having landed at Dalcross and made arrangements for refuelling, arrived at the Station Hotel, Inverness, in a taxi. There had been no suggestion of flying back to London that night. On giving his name when booking rooms for himself and Bertie, he was informed there was a telephone message for him. The reception clerk took it from a rack behind him. Having explained why they had no luggage, Biggles opened it.

'From Ginger,' he told Bertie. 'He's flying Gaskin up. They'll join us here. That's all right with me if that's how he wants it, but I can't imagine what he hopes to do. However . . . I need a wash and brush up. Meet you in the dining-room in ten minutes. Bring the map with you.'

'I've been doing some thinking,' said Bertie, when presently they met in the dining-room for an overdue meal. 'Was it necessary to tell those people we were coppers? Surely that was enough to put them on their guard.'

'That was the intention. In the first place they'd think twice before they started any rough stuff when we talked of searching their machine. We needed authority for that. Secondly, they'll have to do some hard thinking before they decide on their next move. Thirdly, as we've left them in peace they may kid themselves we were satisfied with their explanation.'

'But you aren't?'

'Not by a long chalk. I laid a little trap to find out if they are as innocent as they pretend. I said we'd go on to Dalcross. If they are the people we're after they'll be anxious to know where we are. The first thing they'll do is ascertain if we did really go to Dalcross. I arranged at the airport for a phone call to be put through to me here should anyone make enquiries about us.'

Bertie nodded. 'I get it. If they make enquiries it'll

support your belief that they are the crooks.'

'Exactly. Why else should they bother about us?'

'You didn't tell them your name, so how can they enquire?'

'It wasn't necessary. They'd note the registration letters of our machine. That's all they'd need.'

'Fair enough,' agreed Bertie. 'But I'm still in the dark. They got away in an aircraft. It didn't land on the way here. I'm prepared to swear there was no money in that aircraft when I went over it. How could that happen?'

'There's only one answer to that. When they realised they were being followed, as we know they did because the pilot said so, they dropped the suitcase overboard.'

'In that case it's going to take a bit of finding.'

'Perhaps. But they wouldn't be such fools as to drop it where they themselves would have a job to find it. They'd go low and dump it near an unmistakable landmark. I fancy I know the one they chose. We'll have a look. We shall need a car. When we've finished eating go out and hire a four-seater, something with horses in its engine. I'll wait for you in the lounge. I want to have a close look at the map.'

'If they dropped the swag aren't you afraid they'll recover it while we're sitting here?'

'There is a risk of that, but a small one. It wouldn't be easy to find a suitcase in broad daylight, let alone in the dark. It's my guess they'll wait for daylight.'

'Okay.' Bertie finished his meal and went out. 'See you later.'

An hour later he joined Biggles, who was studying the map in the lounge. 'I've got a Vanguard,' he said. 'It's outside.'

'Good. That should suit us.'

'And what now?'

'We'd better wait for Gaskin or he'll be peeved. No matter. There's no hurry. We can't do anything in the dark.'

They were still waiting, talking the matter over, when a page came in to say Biggles was wanted on the phone. Biggles took the call. When he came back he said, with a note of satisfaction in his voice: 'That was the airport. A man rang up to ask if an Auster of our registration had landed there and, if so, was it still there? Why should anyone be interested in our movements? I'll give you one guess. Who, in Scotland, except the people we followed, knows our registration?'

'Jolly good. Then it begins to look as if we're on the right track.'

It was well after eleven when Inspector Gaskin, with Ginger and a sergeant named Green, walked in. All were in plain clothes.

'Where are they?' demanded Gaskin, belligerently.

'Take it easy,' reproved Biggles. 'There's no need to get burnt up.'

'There's plenty of need,' answered Gaskin grimly. 'That young constable they shot was a friend of mine. I persuaded him to join the Force. Inside a year and he's shot dead. I shan't rest till these devils are caught.'

'Sit down and order yourself a drink. Relax.'

'Do you know where they are?'

'I think so.'

'Then why didn't you nail 'em when they landed?'

'I had nothing to nail 'em on – apart from a minor civil flying offence. If you'll listen I'll tell you what happened. We picked up a plane which we had reason

56

to think was the one the crooks used to give you the slip. We followed it here. When it landed, on a field said to be a flying club, we followed it in. There were three men on board, one, of course, being the pilot. We searched the aircraft; we found nothing.'

'Then you must have followed the wrong plane.'

'I don't think so.'

'Then what's the answer?'

'When they realised they were being followed by another plane they dropped the money.'

'Did you see it fall?'

'No.'

'Then how the hell can we hope to find it?'

'With any luck we should catch 'em when they go to recover it.'

'And where's that likely to be?'

'I have an idea. I may be wrong, but it's the best I can do. It's safe to suppose they'd drop the stuff within reasonable distance of where they knew they were going to land. For obvious reasons they wouldn't choose a built-up area. They'd take the loneliest place they could find. To be sure of marking the spot they'd have to fly low – really low. They tried to lose us in a cloud layer, but we went through after them. When we spotted them they were flying low, almost touching the treetops of a forestry plantation. I can think of only one possible reason, in the circumstances, why they should go so low, particularly as they had to grab altitude afterwards to reach their objective.'

'They might have been trying to elude you.'

'They had already tried that and failed. This, I must admit, is only surmise, but I'd say that with me on their tail they didn't want to land with what they had with them.'

'So they dropped it.'

'That's what I think. Duncan, the pilot, was born in these parts. He must know the country. That plantation fills the requirements. It's near a road; not far from the landing ground; and it's an unmistakable landmark.'

'Could you find the place? I mean on the ground.'

'Of course. I've been checking it on the map. It's about twenty miles from here. The road is the one that runs from the coast to the Spey. The last part of it runs across open moor. There are several forestry plantations, but the one we want is marked by two small pools of water. It's about half a mile long and a hundred yards wide with three fire breaks running across it.'

'Then what are we waiting for?'

'Daylight.'

'What's wrong with going now?'

'Have you ever tried getting through a Forestry Commission plantation – in daylight?'

'I can't say as I have.'

'If you had you'd know it wouldn't be easy to find a herd of elephants. To find a suitcase in the dark would be next to impossible. Apart from anything else you'd tear yourself to pieces on the deadwood undergrowth.'

'Then how will the crooks find the case?'

'They have the advantage of knowing exactly where they dropped it, if in fact they did that. They'd be able to mark the precise spot where it hit the ground. That, I think, is why they went down to treetop level.'

'Why not go to their landing field and catch 'em there?'

'They may not be there now. Even if they were it's unlikely they'd have the money, so you'd have no case.

We want them with the stolen money on them. My suggestion is, we go to the plantation and wait for them to arrive. That should be soon after daylight. I've laid on a car. It's outside. If they don't turn up—well, we can look for the case ourselves. If we can't find it we shall have to do some more thinking. By the way, did you put a gun in your pocket?'

'You bet I did. Sergeant Green has one, too. I'm taking no chances with gunmen who are already wanted for murder.'

'Good. Then we might as well move off. It might take us a little while to locate the place and we ought to be in position by dawn.'

On any night of the year a Scottish Highland moor is not the most cheerful place in the world. At two o'clock in the morning, under a lowering sky, it presents a melancholy picture indeed—peopled, according to local legend, by kelpies and other mischievous spirits. So Biggles and his party found it as they crossed the silent undulating expanse of heather to their objective. An occasional solitary wind-distorted pine, standing black and stark against the colourless background, did nothing to brighten an atmosphere now sinister with an unseen menace. Nothing moved. It was as if all life had died. The only sound was the purr of the car engine and the bite of tyres on a gritty road. A reed-girt pool lay like a sheet of black mirror glass.

'That's the second tarn,' said Biggles, dropping his speed to dead slow. 'This must be it.' He stopped by what appeared to be a black wall with a ragged top. The plantation. He switched off all lights.

They all got out and for a few moments stood still,

listening. Complete silence greeted them.

'I don't see another car,' said Biggles softly, peering into the gloom. 'There's no one here. If anyone was moving within a mile of us we'd hear them on a night like this. And remember, they'd hear us, so keep quiet.'

'Strewth! What a country,' muttered Gaskin.

'You're not seeing it at its best,' murmured Biggles.

'I meant for a crook to hide up.'

'You couldn't be more wrong. A stranger is a marked man. People naturally wonder what he's doing.'

Gaskin jerked a thumb at the plantation. 'We shan't find anything in this.'

'I thought you'd think that when you saw it.'

Actually, the trees were not yet half-grown and therefore not much taller than a man; but they were conifers, and as is usual with Forestry Commission plantations had been set so close together that their branches intermingled. Now, from ground level, it could be seen that the wood was on a slight slope.

Biggles went on. 'The first thing is to get the car out of sight. That would tell anyone arriving we were here. Ginger, take it along a little way. Try to find a place just off the road, but be careful not to get bogged. Leave the lights off.'

Ginger was away about five minutes. They waited for him.

'Now what?' asked Gaskin. 'I'm not used to this sort of country. Cities are my line. In London I know where I am.'

'The people who live here know where they are, too. Never mind. All we can do is wait. Wait till there's enough light for us to see what we're doing. We might as well sit down.'

They found seats in a small, sand depression that had once been a rabbit warren. Gaskin took out his pipe.

'Don't strike a match,' requested Biggles, sharply. 'A light would be seen for miles. The people we're waiting for might be cunning enough to do some exploring on foot before they bring their car along.'

Gaskin grunted and put the pipe back in his pocket.

It was a long time before the first pallid streak of light appeared in the east to announce the approach of another day. As it grew stronger Biggles surveyed the scene. 'It's time we were getting into position,' he decided. 'Chief, I suggest you and I stay here. Ginger, you and Sergeant Green move, say, forty yards or so along the topside of the wood. Keep your heads down. Bertie, you take the lower side. Keep close enough to hear if anything happens. We should hear a car coming if we don't see it. It may not have its lights on.'

'What makes you think they'll come to this end of the wood?' asked Gaskin, as the others moved off.

'When we spotted the machine it was approaching from this end. I imagine they used the road as a guide. They'd need one. Knowing they were coming back, they wouldn't be likely to drop the case further from the road than was necessary.'

'I'd say they aren't coming or they'd be here by now,' said Gaskin, looking about now there was sufficient daylight.

'Sit still and put the brake on your impatience,' returned Biggles. 'This is a cat and mouse game. We're the cat.'

Half an hour passed. It was now broad daylight.

'They're not coming,' declared Gaskin. 'If they were they'd have been here before this. There was a lot of money in that case, too much to leave lying around. We should have grabbed them at their landing ground.'

'It's unlikely we would have found them there – unless, of course, we've been on the wrong track all along. I told you I was working on a theory, the only one I could find to fit the case.'

'Instead of sitting here getting stiff I feel like settling the argument by searching the wood. It wouldn't take long.'

'All right. Go ahead. I wish you joy. Don't make a noise about it.'

Gaskin got up and his burly figure forced a passage into the thickset saplings.

More time passed. A good deal of crashing and twig-snapping told of Gaskin still searching. Biggles did not move. He was beginning to fear his plan had failed. Then Gaskin reappeared, dishevelled, carrying his bowler hat, his face red and covered with scratches. 'It's no use,' he growled, sinking down beside Biggles and mopping his face tenderly with a handkerchief. 'Talk about looking for a needle in a haystack. It'd take a month o' Sundays to do that jungle properly.'

With a sudden movement Biggles put out an arm and forced the inspector flat on his back. 'Don't move,' he hissed. 'I hear a car. It may be them.'

In an instant the situation had changed. A car roared up and came to a skidding stop. Through a fringe of heather Biggles saw two men get out, making a lot of noise, apparently in a desperate hurry. They spoke loudly, as if precautions were unnecessary.

'No one here,' said one. 'If there was we'd see the car. It's okay. Come on. I can go straight to the place. It won't take a minute.'

They crashed directly into the plantation, leaving no one in the car.

'Two of 'em,' Biggles told Gaskin who, being on his back, had seen nothing. 'The pilot isn't with 'em. I didn't think he would be. He didn't like the sound of murder. I saw his face.'

'Stiffen the crows!' muttered Gaskin. 'They're pretty sure of themselves, making all that din. We'll wait here and catch 'em with the stuff on 'em when they come out. What about Bertie and the others? Should we fetch 'em?'

'They must have heard the car arrive, so they should be working their way towards us.'

Gaskin put on his bowler. He took a revolver from his pocket, examined it and replaced it. 'I'm ready,' he said grimly.

It took the bandits twenty minutes to find their loot. They could be heard crashing about, calling to each other and swearing. A shout of triumph announced the success of their search. Snapping twigs, coming nearer, betrayed the line of their return. Presently they appeared, one carrying a suitcase, within a dozen paces of where Biggles and Gaskin were crouching.

Gaskin rose up like an avenging angel. 'All right,' he said sternly. 'Don't let's have any fuss. Ah! So it's you . . . .'

He got no further. The man with the case dropped it with a vicious curse and in a flash had whipped out an automatic. Seeing what was going to happen, Biggles snatched up a handful of sand from a rabbit scrape and flung it in his face. This may have saved Gaskin's life. The gun spat, and from the way the detective flinched Biggles knew he had been hit. Before the bandit could fire again Gaskin had pulled out his revolver and shot him. The man folded up and went down on his knees.

The other bandit tried to back into the trees, shooting wildly, but Sergeant Green and Ginger now appeared on the scene and cut him off. Ginger grabbed the arm that held the gun. Green, who was a big man, had his own method. His arms went round the bandit's chest and he squeezed, crushing the breath out of him until he gasped. Then he took a short pace back. His fist flew out. It met the bandit's chin with a crack like a pistol shot. The man went over backwards as if struck by a charging bull. He lay still.

Biggles had run to Gaskin, who stood with blood running down his face. 'Where did he hit you?' he asked anxiously.

'Forget it. Just nicked my cheek, that's all, thanks to you.'

The bandit he had shot was sitting up, holding a shoulder, cursing luridly. Bertie, who had arrived, picked up his gun.

'Pipe down, you rat,' grated Gaskin. 'I've been waiting for you for a long time. Get the bracelets on 'em, Green. I'm taking no chances.'

'We'd better get to a doctor,' put in Biggles, practically. 'Fetch our car, Ginger. We shall need both.'

Gaskin picked up the suitcase. He looked inside. 'All complete,' he said. 'Bring 'em along.'

So ended a chase that had started in the south of England and ended in the north of Scotland.

Little more needs to be said. The bandit Gaskin had shot soon recovered, but to no purpose, for after their trial and conviction both men paid the maximum penalty for the murder of the police constable. Habitual criminals, with records of violence, they had no real defence. Ballistic experts were able to prove that the gun which had killed the policeman was the one carried by the man who had wounded Chief Inspector Gaskin. When arrested, both men still had in their pockets the stockings they had used in the raid to cover their faces.

What happened to the pilot of the getaway plane was a mystery never solved. As soon as the bandits had been lodged in jail the police went straight on to the so-called flying club landing ground. There was no one there. Duncan, the ex-RAF officer, had gone, presumably in the plane, since it was missing. Biggles was of the opinion that rather than risk a charge of murder he had abandoned his associates and fled abroad.

He may have tried to do this, but if so he failed; for a month later the remains of the aircraft were washed ashore on the Dutch coast, the machine obviously having been forced down in the sea either through engine failure or shortage of petrol. The body of the pilot was never found. Nothing more was heard of him, so it seems likely he was drowned.

So, how he had come to work for the bandits, and whose idea it was to use an aircraft for escape, could never be ascertained. But, as Biggles remarked, it was not important. The scheme had failed.

Chapter 4

A MATTER OF CO-OPERATION

The door of Air Police Headquarters at Scotland Yard was opened and the burly figure of Detective-Chief Inspector Gaskin CID appeared. He glanced around, and seeing only Air-Sergeant Bertie Lissie, enquired: 'Where's everyone?'

Bertie answered: 'Biggles is with the Chief; Algy is still in India and Ginger's gone to London Airport for a natter with Her Majesty's officers of Customs and Excise. Can I do anything for you?'

'How long is Biggles likely to be?'

'He should be back any minute.'

Gaskin knocked out his pipe into the palm of his hand and dropped the crumbs of carbonised ash into an ashtray.

A minute later Biggles breezed in. 'Hello, Chief,' he said briskly. 'What load of trouble are you hawking round?'

Gaskin did not smile. 'Pug Donovan is back in circulation.'

'What am I supposed to do, burst into tears?'

'It's no joke. You can't know him. He's an ugly customer in every sense of the word. He's a bruiser. Fists like cauliflowers and fingers like blunt parsnips.'

'Quite a greengrocer. I take it he's been away.'

'Close on a year. Last night I had a tip he was in a pub called the Frigate in Stepney. By the time I got there . . .'

'He'd gone.'

'Are you telling this story or am I?' demanded Gaskin.

'I'm only trying to hurry you along to the point where you think I may come into the picture. I assume that's why my office stinks of that shag tobacco you burn in your pipe.'

'I want to know how, with every sea and airport watching for him, he got back into the country.'

'So that's it. How should I know?'

'Reckoning he didn't *swim* the Channel, he must have got someone to fly him over. Here's his mug.' Gaskin put a photograph on the desk. 'No one could miss spotting a gorilla with a dial like that.'

'Not exactly a pin-up boy,' agreed Biggles. 'There's nothing I can do about it.'

'You admit he might have got in that way?'

'I've told you before, and I've told the Commissioner, I can't prevent this sort of thing. In wartime you can shoot down an intruder who refuses to identify himself. In peacetime, no. Why do you want this nasty piece of work?'

'He could tell us where he's got sixty thousand quid in notes tucked away. I knew he'd come back for it some day. I've been waiting.'

'Is he the only man who knows where it is?'

'Another old lag, also an Irishman, named Spud O'Connel, might know.'

'You don't know where he is, either?'

'I know all right. He's doing a seven-year stretch on Dartmoor. He won't open his mouth.'

'He would if I made the laws of the land.'

'Oh, and how would you manage that?' Gaskin was

mildly sarcastic.

'I'd sentence these wide boys, who have their swag hidden away, to stay in the nick until they coughed it up.'

Gaskin nodded. 'You may have something there. But you try getting the law changed. Pug and Spud busted a bank in Pimlico. They were careless enough to leave their paw marks. We arrived two minutes too late. We picked up Spud, but Pug got away. He was seen in Paris the next day.'

'Had he got a passport?'

'Yes, although it's out-of-date now. He must have caught the next boat. He wouldn't have been so crazy as to try to get the swag through both British and French Customs. No. He dumped it somewhere and then made his getaway. Knowing we were hot on his trail, he must have been pretty smart about it. Whether the stuff was hidden before he and Spud parted company I don't know for sure, but Spud would know where it was going because that would be arranged beforehand. They've worked together for years.'

'Why didn't Spud stay with Pug?'

'Spud hadn't got a passport. In any case, with us after them they'd know it would be safer for 'em to part company. So, like I say, Pug managed to get away, but we got Spud the next day. He won't squeal. He knows that if he did, when he'd served his time Pug would be waiting to slice him up. Now Pug's come back here to collect the loot. He won't dare to stay here. He knows we'll be waiting. His problem will be to get the money out of the country, but if I'm any good at guessing he'll have got that organised before he came over. I reckon he'll go back to France the same way as he got here – by air.'

'Meaning that as soon as Pug has collected the swag, the aircraft that brought him here will come back to fetch him?'

'That's it. Knowing he daren't show his face, he won't stay here longer than he can help, so I haven't got much time.'

'Why do you think he risked going to the Frigate?'

'It's a regular meeting place for these rats. That's why I keep an eye on it. I'd say Pug went there to get news of Spud. Being abroad, he might not know what had happened to him.'

'By now he'll know he's on the Moor with another five or six years to go.'

'Of course.'

'Do you think Pug has a hide-out in London?'

'Bound to have, or he wouldn't have dared to come here.'

'Would Spud know where it is?'

'Probably. That doesn't mean they'd trust each other very far if there's cash in the kitty.'

'I imagine if news reached Dartmoor that Pug was back the word would soon go round?'

'Every old lag would know inside an hour. They have their own system of signalling. They'd also know that sixty thousand has never been recovered.'

'That should throw Spud into a fever. He'll imagine Pug getting away with the lot.'

'No doubt of that. What's in your mind?'

'This may sound a bit unorthodox, but why not give Spud a chance to escape? He'd make a beeline either for the cash or the hide-out. All you'd have to do would be to follow him. He'd tell you all you want to know.'

Gaskin looked incredulous. 'Are you kidding? Put that up to the powers that be and they'd send for a psychoanalyst to examine your head.'

'I was afraid you'd say that,' sighed Biggles.

'Well, will you do something about this air angle?' pleaded Gaskin.

'Without promising results I'll lay on everything in my power to see Pug doesn't depart by air without saying goodbye to us. Meanwhile, you'd better go on looking for him.'

'You can bet I shall do that,' replied Gaskin grimly. 'If I have any luck I'll let you know right away.'

After the detective had gone Biggles looked across at Bertie and shook his head. 'Fancy trying to find one particular rat in all the holes there are in London.'

'Could he be right about Pug getting here by air?'

'I suppose so. It would depend on the sort of brain he has and if he could find a pilot willing to take a chance. Only another crook, one able to fly and with an aircraft at his disposal, could undertake the job. If such a man existed, and knew Pug had sixty thousand smackers waiting to be collected, he'd probably take it on. Crooks all understand one language – money.'

'It's hard to see what we can do about it. How are we going to find this crooked pilot, assuming there is one?'

'There's one line of approach we might try. Apparently Pug has been lying low in France, probably Paris. Run over and ask Marcel Brissac if he has a pilot in his records, not in prison, who, given sufficient money, might be able to lay his hands on an aeroplane.'

'And if he has?'

'Get the details. Find out who he is, where he is, and what he's doing at the moment. No doubt Marcel will

70

help you. Whether you stay over there or come back home will depend on what you learn. Take plenty of money with you in case you decide to stay.'

'If I find this man and see him take off I phone you. Is that it?'

'Not exactly. That might be all right in daylight, but I can't see anyone trying to slink in in broad daylight; it would be far more likely to happen after dark; yet after dark I wouldn't have a clue as to where he intended to land. Unless you were able to check his course, and I wouldn't hold out much hope of that, he might touch down anywhere between Kent and Land's End. That's the difficulty. But we won't try to jump that fence until we come to it. For a start see Marcel and find out if he can help us. There's no time to waste. Pug might slip away any day. It depends on what arrangements he has made, or has in mind.'

'I'll press on, then,' said Bertie, getting up. 'You'll be hearing from me, or if not from me, from Marcel. So long.'

Rather more than two hours later Bertie landed at Le Bourget, where his police and Interpol identity cards waived the usual formalities. Having seen his Auster in safe hands, he took a taxi into Paris, where at police headquarters he had the good luck to find Marcel Brissac, Biggles' French opposite number, in his office. Greetings exchanged, he explained his mission.

Said Marcel, thoughtfully: 'This man Donovan may be the elusive character the police have been hunting for a long time. We know he entered the country; the Security Officers on the train stamped his passport; but there is no record of him leaving. He must have changed his name. As far as we know he has done nothing wrong, but he should have applied for permission to stay.'

'Well, if this man is the one we're after he isn't in France at this moment, although we have reason to think he may soon return,' answered Bertie. 'The real point is this. How is he able to move from France to England without going through the usual channels? Do you know of a pilot who would undertake to fly him across? If so, how did Donovan get in touch with him?'

Marcel made a typical French gesture. 'That would not be so difficult. You know what they say about birds of a feather. If Donovan didn't know the Paris underworld he would soon find his way into it. These rats can smell each other's holes from a long distance.'

Bertie agreed. 'The question is, do you know of one who would, or could, fly Donovan to England? Remember, a lot of money is involved.'

Marcel thought for a little while. Then he shook his head slowly. 'No. I know of no crook who is a pilot, or has an aeroplane. That does not mean there isn't one. We know that smuggling by air goes on all the time, but so far I cannot catch anyone. How does one stop an aeroplane for questioning?'

'We're up against the same difficulty.'

Marcel's expression changed. 'But wait! A thought comes to me. There is just a chance this may answer a question for me. *Écoutez.* There is a small aviation company which works from a private aerodrome near Chantilly. It is run by two partners, one French, one British. It smells – how do you say? – fishy. These men spend much money. Where, I ask myself, does it come from? No doubt they cheat the tax collector, but that does not explain the business. They say they do private hire work, to anywhere – England, Switzerland, Italy, Spain . . . But with good regular services everywhere, who must have a special plane? And usually at night. They started with one plane, an old Berline Breguet. Now they have a new Aubert Gigale-Major, a four-seat monoplane for touring. This costs much money. Another thing makes me smell fish. One goes often to a shady *bistro* named The Black Fox near the Place de la Bastille. Why do they go there? This is a place where crooks meet?'

'You think perhaps birds of a feather. . . ?'

'*Tiens – tiens. Exactement.* They have been seen with heads together talking to Armand Picot.'

'Who's he?'

'Once the King of the Black Market, now, I suspect, although I cannot prove it, the Prince of Smugglers. These two pilots of Chantilly are clever. I watch, but still I don't know what they do.'

'What are their names?'

'Desmond Grattan and Jacques Montelle.'

'You think they may specialise in doing work for crooks, or flying them when they have to move quickly? Perhaps Donovan.'

'Who can say? It is possible. They make too much money for honest men. Yet I cannot stop them flying.'

'Grattan sounds Irish. Why is he allowed to work in France?'

'He was in your Air Force in the war. He was shot down and hidden by the Resistance. After the war he was allowed to remain in France because he wishes to marry a French girl. Always he wears a little pair of wings in his buttonhole.'

'Why?'

'I do not know. Perhaps he is proud to be a pilot. Perhaps to let people know he is one. Montelle was in the French Air Force. He, too, was shot down, and carries on his face a scar which he tries to hide with a beard.'

'I'd like to see these two air operators. I have no excuse for landing at Chantilly, but there's no reason why I shouldn't have my evening meal at the *bistro*.'

'Take care, *mon ami*. It is not a safe place for a man with money in his pocket – unless he is known as one of the crooked fraternity.'

'I'll look in this evening.'

'What will you do?'

'Matter of fact, I haven't worked that out yet. I may not have to do anything.'

'*Pourquoi?*'

'I'm wearing an RAF tie. That might serve as an introduction to Grattan if he's there. You might ring Biggles for me and tell him what I'm doing.'

'But certainly.'

'Thanks, old boy.'

With that Bertie departed. He had a good lunch and devoted the rest of the afternoon locating and surveying, from the outside, the *bistro* Marcel had named, The Black Fox. It was typical of such establishments, a few tables for meals with a bar on one side. Later he had a cup of coffee and waited for night to fall before proceeding with his scheme. In fact, he had no clear-cut plan beyond having a look at one or both of the men of whom Marcel was suspicious. For the rest he was relying more on chance to pick up information that might be helpful. In the event luck was with him, although what happened was perhaps a natural consequence of the situation.

As it was still early there were not many people in the place when he entered, but by the time he had sipped a drink, had seated himself at a table and was reading the menu – for he intended having his evening meal there – customers were arriving almost too fast for him to give them individual scrutiny.

He gave his order to a weary-looking waiter and, still looking about him, was half-way through his meal when he noticed a man at the bar, whom he had not seen come in, taking more interest in him than seemed necessary. He thought he knew the reason when he saw in the man's buttonhole a tiny pair of gold wings. It must be Grattan, he decided. He took no further notice, but as he sat lingering over his coffee the man appeared beside him, and seating himself remarked in English:

'Hello. I spotted your RAF tie. What are you doing in a dive like this?'

'I'm minding my own business,' Bertie told him coolly.

'All right. There's no need to be snooty. I served in the RAF. Staying long in Paris? I live here now, and might be able to give you some tips.'

'Thanks, but I shall not be here a minute longer than I can help. I'm on my way home.'

'Then what are you doing here?'

'Neither BEA nor Air France has a seat until to-morrow.'

'What's wrong with the night boat train?'

'I'd rather not travel by train.'

Grattan winked. 'Got something in your luggage. . .?'

'I have no luggage.'

'Where have you come from?'

'If you must know I ran into a spot of bother down

75

south. I popped in here to be out of the way.'

'What was the trouble?'

'Read the papers and you may guess.'

'So now you're in a hurry to get across the Ditch?'

'Don't be so damned inquisitive.'

'All right – all right. It merely struck me I might be able to help you.'

Bertie frowned. 'Why should you?' Things were going the way he hoped, but he was anxious not to appear eager.

'Got any money?'

'What's that to do with you?'

'I could get you to England tonight, if that's what you want. But I don't work for nothing.'

'And just how would you do that?' enquired Bertie cynically. 'You got a yacht or something?'

'Better. I could fly you across.'

'Don't waste my time. In what?'

'A plane. What the hell do you think? It happens I run an aviation business. I'm always willing to help an old comrade – for a consideration, of course.'

'You're not serious?'

'Why should I waste my time fooling someone I don't know?'

'What do you call a consideration?'

'Two hundred quid, English or French – it's all the same to me.'

Bertie pulled a face. 'That's a bit steep for a short trip.'

'I don't charge by the mile, but by the risks.'

'Two hundred's about all I have on me, and I'd need some of that when I got to the other side.'

'If you care to wait till tomorrow night I'd do it for a

hundred, flat. Fifty when we start and the rest when we're across.'

'What's the difference?'

'I've got to go across tomorrow night anyway, to pick up a passenger.'

This, thought Bertie, was better and better. 'I don't want to arrive at an airport.'

'Don't be damn silly. Do you think I do? I'd put you down not too far from London. I could have a taxi waiting. You'd need twenty-five quid for the fare.'

'Do I need a taxi?'

'Unless you feel like walking nine miles to the nearest station and waiting there for the first train in the morning. Well, how about it?'

'The best I can do is a hundred and fifty, part English pound notes and part in francs. That'd leave me twenty-five for the fare and a bit in my pocket.'

'Okay. Call it a deal. Say a hundred when we get to the plane and the rest when we're across. That's fair enough.'

Bertie agreed. 'What's the drill, exactly?'

'You stay here. I have some phone calls to make, one to London for your taxi. At twelve midnight I pick you up in my car and we go to the airfield. The plane will be waiting. That's all there is to it.'

'Where do we land?'

'You'll see when we get there.' Grattan got up. 'See you later.'

It need hardly be said that Bertie was well satisfied. This was better than he could have hoped. It seemed too good to be true. From what had been said, unless he was lying, which seemed pointless, Grattan and his

77

partner were obviously running an illegal service, even if, as a cover, there was a legal side to their business. Marcel's suspicions had been well founded. He was tempted to ring him to tell him so but decided not to risk it in case he was being watched. That could come later. So all he could do was have more coffee and watch the customers, wondering how many of them were criminals. Anyhow, it was clear that this was where Grattan did the shady side of his business. No one molested him.

A little before twelve Grattan came in. Without sitting down he simply said: 'Come on. We're all set.'

They went out. A fast-looking sports car was waiting. Grattan only paused to say, 'I hope you've got that money on you. God help you if you've been wasting my time.'

'Don't worry. You'll get it,' answered Bertie. 'Want to see it?'

'I'll take your word for it till we get to the plane.'

The car sped away, heading north, as Bertie had anticipated, this being the direction of Chantilly. During the twenty-mile drive that followed there were moments when he told himself that whatever else happened that night he would not be in greater danger, such risks did Grattan take. No names had been mentioned, but he had no doubt about the identity of his companion. He was relieved when the car turned on to a secondary road and then through a gate to come to a halt near an aircraft which, with airscrew ticking over, stood outside a hangar. A man made a signal.

Grattan turned to Bertie and held out his hand. Bertie, who had already bundled the agreed amount, passed it over. Grattan counted the money and put it in his pocket. That was all. In a matter of minutes the machine was in the air. It was a side-by-side two-seater. It showed no lights. Looking down, Bertie could see the vague shape of the famous race-course of Chantilly, with its stands and stables.

Of the flight that followed nothing need be said. Grattan flew like an experienced pilot. The compass showed a course a trifle west of north. The Channel was crossed without the slightest trouble at 4,000 feet. Grattan glided across the coast, and in fact did not touch the throttle again before going down to a smooth landing on English soil. They got out. Bertie handed over the rest of the money, and looking about him saw to his surprise they were on an aerodrome – from the absence of lights, one not in use.

'Where the deuce are we?' he exclaimed.

Grattan chuckled. 'If you served in the war you should remember the Easterhangar emergency landing ground. They packed it up when it was no longer wanted, which suits me fine. Here comes your car. Don't forget the twenty-five nicker. That's the arrangement. There's no need for me to stay. I'll get back. So long. If you ever want me again you know where to find me.' Grattan got into his seat and disappeared into the night sky.

The car, an ordinary taxi, showing no lights, drew up. 'Here we are,' said a voice. 'Pay in advance is the rule.'

Bertie handed over twenty-five pounds and with a feeling of unreality got in. This was too easy to be believed.

'Where do you want me to drop you off, guv'nor?' asked the driver.

'You mean in London?'

'I ain't going anywhere else.'

'Trafalgar Square suit you?'

'Okay by me.'

The car moved off, the driver switching on his lights as soon as they were on the main road, and an hour later, for there was no traffic, put him down in Trafalgar Square. Still slightly dazed by the ease and simplicity of the trip Bertie took its number as it continued on its way. Taking a taxi from the rank in Leicester Square, he reached the flat a little after three a.m. Trying not to disturb the others, he let himself in quietly and was making a cup of tea in the kitchenette when Biggles, in his pyjamas, appeared in the doorway. 'I thought I heard something,' he said. 'What the devil are you doing here? I expected you to be away two or three days.'

Bertie smiled. 'I've just come from Paris by a service specially laid on for me.'

'What are you talking about? Didn't you fly home in the Auster?'

'No. It's still in Paris. Let me get a cuppa and I'll tell you all about it.' Having made the tea, he went through to the sitting-room.

Ginger, putting on his dressing-gown, came in. 'What's going on?'

'Listen, chaps, you're not going to believe this,' said Bertie seriously. 'Has Gaskin picked up Pug?'

'No. Not a sign of him. Don't say you've seen him!'

'I'm hoping to before very long, although this is by no means certain.' Bertie told his story. 'So, while this may not be the route Pug Donovan is using, I seem to have got my hooks in a pretty smart outfit,' he concluded. 'Grattan's coming over again tonight, so we should soon know what he's up to.'

Biggles drew a deep breath. 'Of course, we always realised this sort of thing could go on. Easterhangar. A disused airfield without a guard. It's too easy. We shall have to take up this question of wartime emergency landing grounds. Tonight should provide us with a concrete case to lay before the Commissioner. He can take it up with the Ministry. We'll be waiting for Grattan when he comes. We'll take Gaskin along. I'll tell him to do nothing about the taxi. We can deal with that on the airfield.'

'Will you tell Marcel what goes on?'

'Not yet. We'll get this end buttoned up first.' Biggles looked at Bertie. 'This is your show, so if you want to come with us tonight you'd better finish your tea and get some sleep.'

Shortly before midnight a police car, showing no lights, tucked itself close to the one dilapidated hangar on the silent abandoned airfield. In it were Biggles, Gaskin, Bertie and Ginger. They got out and walked along the cracked and broken perimeter track to a hut above which a windstocking pole stood stark against the sky. The door sagged open, hanging on one hinge.

'We'll wait here,' said Biggles. 'The taxi is pretty certain to use the track for as far as it goes. We'll grab it when it stops. It should be here before the aircraft. Having got the bracelets on anyone who's in the cab, we can keep out of sight in the hut till the machine arrives. Now we'd better keep quiet. Ginger, keep watch from the door. On a still night like this we should hear the taxi coming from a fair distance.'

Said Bertie: 'Weather conditions are the same as last

night. We touched down a little after two o'clock.'

'If Pug arrives in that cab don't forget what I told you about him being a tough customer,' warned Gaskin. 'Being an old-timer I don't think he carries a gun.'

It seemed a long time before anything happened. In fact it was nearly two hours. But at last, speaking from the door, Ginger said quietly: 'Here it comes.'

The taxi, lights switched off, purred to a stop where the track ended a few yards from the hut. For two or three minutes no one got out, but muffled voices indicated the presence of at least two people. Then the door was pushed open and a heavily built man carrying a suitcase got out. The driver stepped down from his seat and joined him.

'I usually wait here till I hear it coming,' he said.

'If you say so,' was the answer. 'Here you are.' Something passed between them.

'It's Pug,' breathed Gaskin. 'Come on.' He strode out with the others close behind.

The fight that followed need not be described. The taxi-driver had soon had enough, but Pug lived up to his reputation as a bruiser. Cursing luridly, he fought like a trapped tiger, and by the time he was over-powered and the handcuffs were on his wrists everyone bore the marks of his flailing fists and boots. However, the odds against him were bound to tell and he was finally secured.

'Any more trouble from you and I'll knock your block off,' panted Gaskin, as with a spare pair of handcuffs he locked Pug to the taxi. 'And keep your mug shut or I'll shut it for you.' No mean pugilist himself, he spoke as if he meant it. 'Let's see what you've got here.' He opened the suitcase, and the light of a torch revealed it to be packed with notes.

There was another wait, but this time only for a matter of minutes. Then the sighing of air over wings announced the approach of a gliding aircraft. Vaguely through the gloom it was seen to touch down and run to a stop about fifty yards away. The pilot jumped down and lit a cigarette. By the time he looked up the police were almost on him. Taken by surprise there was little he could do, which was just as well, for when Gaskin ran his hands over him he found an automatic. What Grattan said when he recognised Bertie need not be repeated.

'The machine can stay where it is for the time being,' decided Biggles. 'I'll ring Marcel when we get back and let him know where it is. Well, I think that's about the lot. Let's get home.'

Chapter 5

BIGGLES CRACKS A NUT

Biggles broke off what he was saying to Ginger when the door of Air Police Headquarters opened and their Chief, Air Commodore Raymond, walked in. He carried a large envelope. 'Sit still,' he said. 'I was passing your room after having a word with Gaskin of "C" Department, so I thought I'd look in instead of calling you to my office. The Yard has been given a toughish nut to crack, and as there may be an aviation angle Gaskin thinks your crackers may do the job better than his.' The Chief pulled up a chair and went on:

'Do you remember, some time ago, an unidentified body being found in peculiar circumstances, in Yorkshire?'

'No, sir. I may have been away, or working on something else at the time.'

'Then I'll give you the facts as far as they're known. A month ago, near the little town of Mapleton in the West Riding, a gardener employed by a certain Colonel Thurburn went to a copse not far from the house to get a bag of leaf mould. Under a tree he found the body of a young man. He reported this to the Colonel, who sent him on his bicycle to Mapleton to inform the police. According to the county pathologist, the body must have been lying where it was found for at least a month. It is still unidentified. The local police now admit they're baffled and have called in Scotland Yard.'

'Where is the body now?'

'Buried. There was no point in keeping it any longer.'

'And where does the aviation angle come in, sir?'

'From the injuries the body had sustained, and the fact that the tree had been damaged from top to bottom, the Divisional Police Inspector is convinced it fell out of the sky. The skull had been fractured, both legs and some ribs were broken, consistent with the theory that the body had fallen from a height. A broken branch, with which apparently it had come in contact, lay near it. There were traces of skin on the bark.'

'Was there anything else to suggest foul play – a bullet wound, for instance?'

'Nothing.'

'Was this man wearing flying kit?'

'No. That's the queer part of it. All he had on was an open shirt, a pullover, trousers, socks and shoes, all of foreign manufacture. No hat, no jacket. Hardly the way you'd expect a man to be dressed for flying.'

'What was in the trouser pockets?'

'Not a thing. There wasn't a single clue that might have led to identification.'

'That *is* queer. Seems as if it might have been deliberate.'

'That's the view taken by Inspector Cole at Mapleton.'

'What has he done about it?'

'Everything possible. The RAF has no one missing. No civil air line operator has lost a passenger. The district has a thin population. Everyone living near has been questioned without result. No one remembers seeing an aircraft – but of course, whether it was accident, suicide or murder, it could have happened after dark.'

Biggles shook his head. 'It wasn't suicide. At all events, I can't see a man bothering to half undress if he intended to destroy himself.'

'It sounds to me more like murder,' asserted the Air Commodore. 'Someone decided to dispose of his victim by throwing the body out of an aircraft.'

'Then why not drop it where no one was ever likely to find it – in the sea, for instance, with a weight to take it to the bottom?' Biggles suggested. 'What do you want me to do, sir? By this time any scent there may have been will be stone-cold. The aircraft from which the man fell, if in fact he did fall, could be anywhere in the world.'

The Air Commodore smiled lugubriously. 'We're expected to find out the name of this man, how the body came to be where it was discovered and who was responsible.'

Biggles looked pained. 'Have a heart, sir. I'm not surprised Gaskin pushed the case along to us.'

'I warned you it would be a tough nut to crack.'

'Unless there's a flaw in the shell it looks as if I shall need a sledge-hammer,' returned Biggles cynically. 'I take it photographs of this curious corpse are available?'

The Air Commodore laid on the desk the envelope he carried. 'Here are some prints. You'll find full physical details written on the backs.'

Biggles withdrew one, and Ginger, looking over his shoulder, saw the face of a man in his early twenties, good-looking in a hard sort of way. Even in death it had a touch of 'class' about it.

'Has this portrait been published?' asked Biggles.

'No. Inspector Cole thought it better not to let it be known yet that the body had been found; hoping, of course, that anyone who knew where it was would return. Well, that's as much as I can tell you. See what you can make of it.'

'Do you happen to know if there is anywhere handy for a plane to get down?'

'Anticipating that question, I asked the inspector. No. It's all rough country. No airfield for miles. You'd better run up by car. You'll need one when you get there, anyway. Anything else?'

'You could save me time by letting the inspector know we're on our way, and ask him to book two rooms for us at a reasonable hotel. We shall have to go home for our kit, so we may arrive late.'

'I'll do that,' promised the Air Commodore, and left the room.

After the door had closed behind him Ginger remarked: 'This looks like being a complete waste of time.'

'I wouldn't say that. All we have to do is sort out the things that don't make sense, put them together, and there we should find the kernel of the nut.'

'None of it makes sense to me.'

'That's where you're wrong,' reproved Biggles. 'Something must make sense or the affair couldn't have happened. No one can live without being known to somebody. Someone, somewhere, must have known this dead man who they say dropped out of the sky. Our job is to find him.'

'Where do we start looking?'

'In Yorkshire. Why was the body found in that particular locality? Of course, it may have been purely accidental; on the other hand there may have been a reason. If there *was* a reason it shouldn't be impossible to find out what that reason was. Now let's get on with it.'

At ten o'clock the following morning Biggles was introducing himself to Divisional Inspector Cole at Mapleton police station. The inspector, a big, square-faced man with a calculating eye, received them cordially, admitting frankly that he had run into a dead end.

'May I start by asking you a few questions?' requested Biggles.

'As many as you like.'

'I take it you've made enquiries locally.'

'Of course. I worked on two lines. First, had anyone noticed a stranger in the district. No one had. Then, concentrating on the flying angle, I asked everyone within a radius of a couple of miles if he or she had seen a plane flying low about the place. That got me nowhere, either. But then, who looks up at a plane nowadays?'

'You're convinced the man, dead or alive, dropped from the air?'

'Everything pointed to it.'

'What houses are there in the area?'

'The nearest is a biggish place known as Mapleton Grange. Apart from that there are a couple of farms and a dozen farm cottages.'

'I believe it was the gardener of the Grange who found the body?'

'That's right. An old fellow by the name of Larwood. He's lived around here all his life. He now works for Colonel Thurburn, a retired army officer who bought the Grange about four years ago. Larwood occupies the lodge at the entrance gate.'

'Who lives at the Grange?'

'Only the Colonel and his wife. They're both getting on for seventy. Larwood's wife helps in the house as a daily woman. I don't think the old people can have much money. When Larwood told the Colonel what he'd found in Foxhole Spinney, as the place is called, the Colonel sent him straight to me. Larwood looked proper shaken, white as a sheet, when he walked in here.'

'And what did you do?'

'Got in my car and went along, leaving word for a doctor and an ambulance to follow on. I found the body lying spreadeagled on its stomach in deep bracken. It had obviously hit the ground hard, even though it had gone clean through an oak tree, tearing off a branch on the way. The state of the body pretty well confirmed what I suspected had happened. It was badly smashed up. I had a good look round, but finding nothing of interest I had the body taken to the mortuary. Naturally, I started enquiries right away, but they haven't got me anywhere. I must admit I'm beaten. Do you want to see the place?'

'No thanks. No doubt you went over the ground thoroughly, so after the lapse of time I'm not likely to find anything fresh. What I'd like to do next, if you don't mind, is have a word with Larwood. We've got our own car.'

'That's all right with me. I've plenty to do, so you won't mind if I don't come with you? The Grange is only a bit over a couple of miles from here.' The inspector marked it on a map that hung on the wall.

'By the way. Did Larwood go back with you to show

you the body?'

The inspector smiled. 'No fear. He said wild horses wouldn't ever drag him near the place again. The spinney is only a clump of trees, so I didn't need him.'

'I'll see you later,' said Biggles, and with Ginger went out to the car.

A quarter of an hour later it ran to a stop at a lodge that guarded the drive to a grey stone house of some size. A woman was hanging out washing.

'Mrs Larwood?' questioned Biggles.

'Yes, sir.'

'I'm a police officer. I'd like a word with your husband. Is he about?'

'He's working in the garden.' Mrs Larwood pointed. 'There he is. Would you like me to fetch him?'

'Don't bother. I'll walk over to him.' Biggles did so and made himself known. 'I'm making enquiries about the body you found. You may be able to help me. I want you to tell me exactly what happened that morning.'

'Yes, sir.' With a foot resting on his spade, in broad Yorkshire dialect the man told his story in his own way, of how he had gone to the spinney for a bag of leaf mould and came upon the body lying in the bracken under a tree. 'The first thing I see was a face staring up at me out o' the bracken,' he concluded. 'I couldn't see much else, the bracken being deep.'

'Did you examine the body?'

'Not me,' was the vehement answer.

'You didn't touch it?'

'I didn't go any closer. There wasn't no need. One look was enough for me. Like I just told you, I could see from the poor chap's face he'd been dead some time. It looked horrible, with dried blood on it. One look and I was off as fast as I could go.'

'You're quite sure about this?'

'I ain't never likely to forget it. I shall see that face for the rest of me days. Proper shook me up, it did.'

'Then what did you do?'

'Went back to the house as fast as my legs could carry me to tell the guv'nor.'

'Where was he?'

'Writing letters in his study.'

'Did you see anyone else?'

'There wasn't no one else to see. Mrs Larwood had gone to Mapleton with Mrs Thurburn to do the shopping, like they do regular, every week.'

'And the Colonel sent you to fetch the police.'

'Right away. I went on my bike.'

'Did you, on the way, tell anyone what you'd found?'

'No. As it happened I didn't see no one. The first person I spoke to was Sergeant Lane at the police station.'

'Then you came back home?'

'That's right.'

'You didn't go back to the body?'

'Not me. I'd seen all I wanted of that. Besides, the police were there by then. I see the car.'

'Was the Colonel here when you got back?'

'Yes, he'd lit a bonfire over there and was raking up the dead leaves. He sometimes lends a hand in the garden when he's nothing else to do.'

'How long do you reckon it was from the time you left here to fetch the police till the time you got back?'

'Must have bin a good hour, I'd say. They kept me some time at the police station, asking questions. Here comes the Colonel now.'

'Thank you, Mr Larwood.' Turning away, Biggles walked forward to meet the owner of the house.

Ginger followed. He saw a tall, clean-shaven, elderly man, with bright blue eyes and close-cropped iron-grey hair, who, when he was young, must have been a handsome, commanding figure. Now, although he maintained his poise he had begun to stoop a little. His face was deeply lined and his expression austere; but his manner, when Biggles introduced himself, was courteous.

'I have been sent to investigate the death of the man found by your gardener, and if possible establish his identity,' went on Biggles. 'Can you spare me a minute?'

'Certainly, although I doubt if I can add anything to what is already known.'

'I came prepared for that, sir. May I ask where you were when Larwood reported what he had found in the spinney?'

'I don't see much purpose in the question, but I was in my study writing some urgent letters.'

'You sent him to fetch the police.'

'Naturally, as I am not on the telephone.'

'What did you do then?'

'The obvious thing. I stood in the garden until I saw the police car arrive.'

'You didn't go to the spinney to confirm what Larwood had told you?'

'To what purpose? Larwood had told me the man had been dead for some time, so there was nothing I could do.'

'So you didn't go near the body?'

'I have already said I waited here to watch for the

police to arrive. I passed the time by doing some work in the garden.'

'I see, sir. I think that's all. I'm much obliged to you. Now I'll be getting along.'

'Can I offer you some refreshment – a glass of sherry, perhaps?'

'No thanks, sir. I must be getting back.'

'As you wish. In that case I'll say good morning to you.'

'Good morning, sir.'

When they were in the car on the way back to Mapleton Ginger asked: 'What do you make of all that – if anything?'

'You heard everything I heard. Work it out for yourself.'

'Where are we going now?'

'To the pub for some lunch.'

'And after that?'

'Tonight I shall go for a stroll. For the moment I'm thinking.'

Ginger looked at Biggles curiously but said no more.

It was half past nine, and a fine moonlit night, when after a substantial Yorkshire meal Biggles announced it was time they were moving on. They wouldn't need the car. A little exercise would do them good.

'Where are we going?' Ginger wanted to know, not unnaturally.

'Only as far as the Grange. I want to have a closer look at something.'

'In the house?'

'In the garden.'

A brisk walk of half an hour took them to the

objective. A cautious reconnaissance revealed no lights either in the lodge or the big house. Ignoring the gate, which had been closed, they got into the grounds by climbing the wall further along. Biggles then walked on as if he knew exactly where he was going. He stopped at a heap of bonfire ash.

'I don't think we shall be disturbed, but you'd better keep watch,' he said softly, and dropping on his knees began groping in the ashes with his fingers.

Presently Ginger said: 'What on earth are you hoping to find?'

'Frankly, I don't know. But there's a chance I may find something that could turn out to be the kernel of the nut we're trying to crack.'

It was some time before he found anything. Twice he stopped, sniffing. 'Smell anything?'

'No.'

'I can, but maybe that's because I'm closer to the ashes than you are.'

A minute later he uttered a curious sound that might have meant anything. He rose to his feet. 'Take a look at this,' he breathed, holding out an object for Ginger to see. It was a metal ring about three inches in diameter.

'What the deuce is it?' asked Ginger.

'You should know,' answered Biggles, putting the ring in his pocket.

'Is that what you were looking for?'

'It certainly was not – but it should have been. But let's get home. I need a wash.'

Ten o'clock the next morning found them, with Biggles carrying a large envelope, at the police station.

Inspector Cole was there, in uniform. 'Well,' he

greeted. 'How are you getting on? Solved the problem yet?'

His expression changed when Biggles answered evenly: 'I think so. I shall be disappointed if I haven't found someone who can tell us the name of the dead man. I'm now going to ask him. I thought you might care to come along.'

Staring hard at Biggles, the inspector reached for his cap. 'You're not pulling my leg?'

'I don't waste my time when there's a job to be done. My car's outside. We'll use that.'

'Where are we going?'

'To the Grange.'

'The *Grange*!'

'I'm pretty sure the gallant Colonel can tell us all we want to know.'

On arrival the door was opened by the Colonel himself. He seemed surprised to see them. Said Biggles: 'Good morning, sir. I'm sorry to trouble you again, but there's one more question I'd like to ask. Can we go somewhere where we shan't be disturbed?'

The Colonel took a hard look at Biggles' face. 'Come through to my study.' He led the way. 'Now, what's the question?' he enquired when they were in the room.

Biggles took a photograph of the dead man from the envelope he carried and placed it on the desk. 'It may save trouble all round if you'll tell us his name.'

The colour drained from the Colonel's face, but he retained his composure. 'What makes you think I might know?'

'You haven't answered my question,' reminded Biggles softly.

No answer.

'Very well, if you won't tell me I shall have to tell you how much I know,' resumed Biggles. 'Why did you lie to the police?'

The Colonel flushed. 'I'm not in the habit of telling lies.'

'In the ordinary way, sir, I'm sure you are not. That's what puzzles me. You told me you did not go near the body lying in the spinney. That was not true. After Larwood had gone for the police you went to the spot. You must have recognised the man or you wouldn't have taken the trouble to remove everything which might have led to identification. You also took away the parachute which, by failing to open, was responsible for the man's death. You hurried home with these things, but were then faced with the problem of disposing of them. You fetched paraffin, poured it over, and set fire to them in the garden. When Larwood returned you raked dead leaves on the fire. But the rip cord ring, being metal, would not burn. It remained in the ashes. I found it last night. I could still smell the paraffin.' Biggles put the ring on the desk. 'Now, who was this man and why did you do it?'

The Colonel looked stricken. 'Do you mind if I sit down? I see I shall have to tell you everything.' A long pause. 'The dead man was my son.'

From Biggles' expression it was clear this was an answer he did *not* expect.

'My son was a bad boy,' went on the Colonel heavily. 'He was expelled from school. He ran away from home and went from bad to worse. I gave him money to go to South Africa. There he murdered a man and fled to South America. Later he returned to Europe. I needn't go into the details, but his demands for money ruined me. I gave him all I could afford, but it had to end. Recently, in trouble in Paris, he demanded a large sum. I hadn't got it, whereupon he wrote a letter threatening to come here and fetch it. Apparently he tried to do that. When I went to the spinney I was unprepared for the shock of seeing him. I had no suspicion. The possibility never occurred to me . . .'

'Why did you act as you did?'

'For two reasons, although I didn't really stop to think. My first impulse was to save my wife any further distress. The boy had already broken her heart. Secondly, to a lesser degree, I hoped to avoid a scandal.'

'Why do you think he parachuted into the country?'

'I can only suppose he thought that if he travelled openly he would be recognised and arrested. He must have known someone who had an aeroplane and persuaded him, or paid him, to fly him over. As there was nowhere for the plane to land he dropped near the house by parachute. It failed to open.' The Colonel buried his face in his hands.

Biggles touched the inspector on the arm. 'That's enough for now,' he said quietly. 'Let's go.'

'What beats me,' said the inspector when they were back at the police station, 'is how you hit on the truth so quickly. It had been staring me in the face for nearly a month.'

'I wouldn't say that. There's an old saying to the effect that if you look at a wood long enough you can't see it for trees. Coming fresh on the scene I could see it more clearly. On the morning the body was found only three people knew about it: Larwood, the Colonel and you, in that order. From what Larwood told me the body must have been lying face up. He could describe the face. There was dry blood on it. He didn't touch the body and that's easy to believe. From what you told me, when you first saw the body it must have been lying face down – on its stomach, you said. The third person involved, the Colonel, said he didn't go near the body. Someone not only went near it, but *moved* it. Who was lying? I could rule you out. Larwood was sent hot-foot for the police and you were on the spot before he got back. That left only the Colonel. A man of that type doesn't lie readily. The unanswered question was, why had he done it?'

'He didn't want the body to be identified as his son.'

'We know that now. There was another pointer. When Larwood ran back to the house to report what he had found the Colonel was writing urgent letters in his study. After Larwood had gone for the police did he finish writing his letters? No. What was more natural than he should go and look at the body? We can imagine the shock. If he was to do anything it had to be there and then. We know what he did. With his wife and Mrs Larwood in Mapleton, and Larwood not yet back, there was no one to see him. When Larwood did get back what was he doing? Finishing his letters? No. He was in the garden stoking a bonfire – hardly what you'd expect in the circumstances. It seemed to me he must have been in a hurry to burn something. What was it?'

'Did you suspect a parachute?'

'No. I had considered a parachute earlier but dismissed it because some of the fabric would have been caught up in the tree. I confess my imagination didn't run to a parachute that had *failed to function*, although had I been wide awake it should have done. When I went to the bonfire I was hoping to find something, anything, that had not been burnt. Of course, when I found a parachute ring the picture was wide open. I was still puzzled about one thing. When Larwood found the body it must have been wearing the parachute. He never mentioned it. I could only conclude he didn't notice it. That's understandable, as it was in deep bracken. Moreover, if it was a seat-type parachute it would be under the body, then lying face up. Larwood said he took one look and bolted.'

'Why did the Colonel take off the parachute?'

'He had to remove the harness to get at his son's jacket to see what was in the pockets. He couldn't leave it lying there. That would have told you the body had been interfered with. So he took it home, with the jacket, and burnt it. This morning I decided to confront him with the ring, trusting that under the influence of shock it would produce the whole truth – which it did. What the old man did was understandable. Whether or not it was pardonable I leave to you. My own feeling is he has suffered enough without being taken to court.'

The inspector nodded. 'I think you're right. The only case against him is withholding information from the police.'

Biggles held out a hand. 'Well, it's all yours. We'll be getting back to London.'

Chapter 6

THE BIRTHDAY PRESENT

'It's about time some of these star private detectives we see on the telly were dropped into the Force so they could try their hand at the real thing. It makes me laugh the way they find clues sticking out like organ stops – which, of course, the police were too dumb to notice.' The speaker was Detective-Inspector Gaskin of Scotland Yard, and in his voice there was more than a hint of sarcasm.

Biggles, who had gone to the canteen, and finding him there had joined him in a cup of tea, smiled sympathetically. 'Don't let it worry you,' he consoled. 'How else would you have the story end? Let the crook get away with it? That wouldn't do.'

'I suppose not. But why make it seem that amateurs are so much smarter than men like me who have spent half their lives learning the business?'

'Maybe there are occasions when they are,' bantered Biggles.

'That's a nice thing to say,' growled the police officer.

'You're not forgetting I'm what you might call an amateur myself,' reminded Biggles. 'I've only become, shall we say, semi-professional by virtue of being an air pilot.'

'What's so wonderful about that?'

'Nothing, unless it is that flying teaches a man to think fast.'

'The trouble is there are too many crooks, and some

of 'em seem to commit crime, even murder, without a motive,' went on Gaskin lugubriously. 'What can you make of such people?'

'What you mean is, how are you to catch 'em?'

'Put it that way if you like.'

Biggles sipped his tea. 'Come on,' he invited. 'Out with it.'

'Out with what?'

'Something's biting you. What is it?'

'All this newspaper criticism because we haven't been able to find the man who knocked this kid Nellie Tomkins on the head. You must have read about it.'

'Only the headline; not the details.'

'Want to hear 'em?'

'If you like. Get 'em off your chest and we'll see if an amateur can make anything of 'em. I take it this has nothing to do with aviation?'

'Nothing at all. And I wish you'd stop pulling my leg. This is murder.'

'Sorry. Go ahead.'

'Nellie Tomkins was twelve. She was the only child of a couple who live in a cottage near Watton, in Hertfordshire, where she went to school. Actually, the cottage is a lodge at the entrance to an estate. Last Monday she was walking home from school as usual, only a matter of a mile or so, when some devil hit her on top of the head and left her dying beside the road. In a matter of minutes she was seen and picked up by a passing motorist. By the time they'd got her to hospital she was dead. That's as much as we know.'

'No clue to the killer?'

'One. If you can call it a clue. A couple of yards from where the body was found lay a box of chocolates which she may have been carrying or holding when she was struck down. Not cheap chocolates, either. It was a two-pound box of high-class stuff, roses on the lid, gold ribbon and so on. The point is, they weren't the sort that could have been bought in the village. In fact, we know they weren't bought anywhere near. That's been checked. Who would give the poor kid such a box of chocolates and why were they left lying beside the body?'

'Had the girl any other injuries?'

'No. She'd simply been coshed with the proverbial blunt weapon.'

'If it comes to that, why was the body left beside the road? Why wasn't it hidden, in a ditch, or behind the hedge, for instance?'

'I can only suppose the murderer was in too much of a hurry to get away. He may have heard the other car coming – the one that found the body. Normally the road, a secondary one, doesn't carry much traffic.'

'What about the man driving the car who found the body?'

'You can rule him out. He happened to be a parson. His wife was with him. They'd been into Hertford to do some shopping. They must have been the first people to come along after the kid was struck.'

'These chocolates. Had the box been opened?'

'No. It was still wrapped in fancy paper, the sort of stuff they use around Christmas time.'

'Were there any signs of a struggle?'

'None. The girl was killed by a single blow that fractured her skull. She wasn't wearing a hat. There was no blood about.'

'There wouldn't be if only one blow was struck. It's a

second blow in the same place that makes the splashes. But you'd know all about that.'

'I suppose you wouldn't care to run down and have a look at the place where it happened?' suggested Gaskin tentatively.

'There doesn't seem much point in it,' said Biggles. 'I take it you made a thorough search of the area?'

'We've combed every yard. I reckoned to find the murder weapon, but nothing has turned up.'

'Could the girl have been accidentally struck by a hit-and-run motorist?'

'No. I considered that. Had she been knocked down by a passing car there must have been bruises on the body. What sort of vehicle could have hit her on the head without making a mark anywhere else?'

'What's your theory, so far?'

'Naturally, at first I thought the murderer must be someone who knew the girl's habit of walking home, and the time; but I had to discard that when all the men I questioned, local men who might have been there, had convincing alibis. Now all I can think is, some devil, presumably a stranger, in a car or on a motor bike, seeing the girl walking alone along the road, stopped her and gave her the chocolates, or offered them to her, hoping she'd go off with him. Obviously she refused, or her body wouldn't have been where it was found. So he coshed her, maybe, if he had a car, intending to take her with him anyway. The trouble is I can't find anyone who remembers seeing a car, or any other vehicle, about that time. Not that that's conclusive. No one pays much attention to a car. The parson who found her didn't see anyone in front of him, although he must have reached the spot within minutes of the kid being knocked down. Can you see anything wrong with that line of reasoning?'

Biggles shrugged. 'I suppose it could have happened that way, but I find it a bit unconvincing. For instance, if the man was a stranger who didn't know the girl, how did it happen that he had a box of chocolates handy – expensive stuff, moreover, that couldn't have been bought locally? That sounds as if he knew what he was going to do; if so, he must have known about the girl.'

'He may not have been looking for Nellie. Maybe he didn't care what girl it was.'

Biggles thought for a moment. 'I'm puzzled about these chocolates. I feel they're the axis about which the whole thing revolves. Did you tell the press about them?'

'No. They were the only clue I had, so I kept it up my sleeve for the time being. Well, there it is. Now the newspapers are creating. Look at the headlines. What are the police doing? Another unsolved murder! etc., etc. What do they think we are – magicians? As I said just now, I'd like to see some of these TV sleuths have a go at this. They always find the answer.'

'I'd say you've got the answer in that box of chocolates if you can winkle it out.'

Gaskin stuffed tobacco into his pipe. 'Perhaps you can tell me how. I've contacted the makers. The box was one of ten thousand made for the Christmas trade and they were distributed from one end of the country to the other. I've been over that damn box a score of times looking for a mark that might tell me something. It's true one corner is dented, but that could have happened a hundred ways, even before it was bought. The outside wrapping and the string were the sort you can buy anywhere.'

'The box must have been handled. What about fingerprints?'

'Nothing but a lot of smudges. The man who last handled the box, before giving it to the kid, must have been wearing gloves. The same with the parson who picked it up. He handed it to his wife. She put it in the car. It was a chilly day and they were both wearing gloves; so you can imagine how many paw marks there were on the box by the time it reached me.'

'You're talking about the outside wrapping. What about the box itself?'

'Oh that. It must have been handled by scores of people, men and women, probably shop girls, before it was sold. You'd expect that. It'd be put on the shelf. Taken down again. Put in the window. Taken in again to show a customer . . . No, that won't get us anywhere. Do you want to have a look at it?'

'No. What could it tell me that it couldn't tell you? I'd rather have a look at the place where the body was found. How far away is the nearest house?'

'A hundred yards. It's the cottage where the poor kid lived. She was in sight of home when she was murdered.'

'The parents heard nothing?'

'Nothing.'

'No car?'

'No.'

'I was thinking, if the child was attacked she'd scream.'

'Her parents told me they didn't hear a sound.'

'Surely there's something queer about that?'

'They were in the kitchen having their tea when it must have happened, expecting Nellie to walk in any minute.'

'I still think there's something odd about this. Of course, with so much noise these days it's always possible to hear something without noticing it. Somehow I can't see any man bashing a girl on the head before she could open her mouth. Let's go and have a look at the place.'

A little more than an hour later, Inspector Gaskin, driving his own car, pulled up at the spot where the tragedy had occurred. 'This is it,' he said.

It was a typical, rather narrow country road, little more than a lane, with a bank topped by a hedge on one side and a grass verge with a hedge beyond it on the other. They got out.'

Gaskin pointed down the road. 'There's the gate of the cottage where the girl lived. What do you make of it?'

'The first thing that strikes me is this,' answered Biggles. 'No man in his right mind would commit murder in broad daylight so close to a house – any house, never mind the one where the girl lived, assuming he knew that. If he had come prepared, and was carrying the chocolates as a bait, why let the girl get so close to a house? There are places that should have suited his purpose better before she got as far as this.'

'He may not have known what he was going to do.'

'Then why did he bring the chocolates?'

'It may be he just happened to have them with him.'

'In which case we may wonder what he intended to do with them in a country lane such as this? Sit on the bank and eat them? All by himself! There may be men who do that sort of thing, but I've never met one. Let's go on a bit.'

They got back into the car and cruised on slowly to a cottage that stood beside the entrance gate to a drive leading into an estate of some size. One side of the drive was bounded by a stand of fine old beech trees. The other side was typical parkland with various isolated trees at intervals.

'This is where the kid lived,' said Gaskin, thumbing the cottage. 'Are you going in to have a word with them?'

'No. What more could they tell me? Poor souls. Why worry them? We shan't find the answer to our problem there.'

At this moment a cock pheasant flew out of the beeches with a cackle of alarm and crossing the drive glided down in the park.

'There's somebody in that wood,' remarked Biggles.

'What about it?'

'Who is it, and what's he doing there?'

'Does it matter?'

'It might. One never knows. I'm prepared to take an interest in anyone wandering about so close to where the girl was killed. Never leave a stone unturned, as they say – even a pebble if it might hide something.'

'There's your answer,' returned Gaskin, with a wan smile as he filled his pipe.

From out of the trees not far away had stepped a well-dressed attractive young woman. After a glance up and down the drive she crossed it and meandered away across the park. Biggles watched her without speaking.

'I can tell you who she is since you're so interested,' offered Gaskin.

'Who is she?'

'Diana Fairfax, daughter of the man who owns the place.'

'How do you know?'

'In the course of my enquiries I went to the big house and had a word with her father, Sir Eustace Fairfax. She was there.'

'Did you go for any particular reason?'

'To check up on the staff, any manservants, who would of course know Nellie.'

'Were there any?'

'One, the butler. He's over seventy, so we can forget him.'

Biggles was still watching the young woman, now wandering back across the park towards them, her eyes on the ground. 'She seems to have lost something,' he observed. 'I wonder what it could be?'

'Why not go and ask her?' suggested Gaskin in a tone of voice that implied he did not expect to be taken seriously.

'Do you know anything about her?'

'Only that she's engaged, and last Monday when I called was her twenty-first birthday. When I went in she happened to be unwrapping her presents.'

'Do you by any chance happen to know who she's engaged to?'

'Yes. Her father mentioned it when I asked him for the names of any men who had recently visited the house. You might know him. He's a lad in the RAF. Flying Officer named Paget. Not the type to murder anyone, let alone a kid like Nellie, if that's what you're thinking.'

'I wasn't thinking on those lines,' answered Biggles. 'As you've already met Diana you might go and ask her what she's looking for.'

Gaskin gave Biggles a long penetrating stare. 'What the devil has it to do with us?'

'As I've said before, one never knows.'

'Do you think you know what it might be?'

'Let's say I have a notion. I could be wrong.'

'Oh, come on. Don't waste time. What *could* it be?'

'Possibly a box of chocolates.'

Gaskin blinked. A frown furrowed his forehead. 'I don't get it.'

'Well, there she is. You might just see if I'm right. It won't take a minute.'

'I'd say you're anything but right – in the head.' Gaskin strode off.

Biggles waited while the detective had a conversation with the girl lasting about five minutes. When Gaskin came back there was a slightly dazed expression on his face.

'Well,' enquired Biggles. 'What's she looking for?'

Gaskin seemed to have difficulty in speaking. 'A box of chocolates,' he breathed. 'Her fiancé rang up to ask her if she'd found the box he'd dropped for her. She's been looking for it ever since. How the devil did you guess?'

A smile spread slowly over Biggles' face. 'Guess? You as good as told me.'

'How do you make that out?'

'By putting together a number of apparently irrelevant details which nevertheless added up to an idea. Monday, the day Nellie was killed, was Diana's birthday. You saw her unpacking her presents. A common present for a girl is a good box of chocolates. Diana is engaged to a flying officer. To my certain knowledge he wouldn't be the first pilot, by a long chalk, to drop a present to his girl from an aircraft. It's so much more romantic than having the postman deliver it. Unfortunately our dashing young airman, Flying Officer Paget, was a bit wide of the target, which I imagine was the lawn in front of the house. The box hit the road, or it would have done if it hadn't landed on the head of that unlucky child. You told me a corner of the box had been dented. No wonder the girl didn't scream. She never knew what hit her. So there we are. It all fitted like a jigsaw. What happened was a million to one chance, but sometimes luck, or fate, has its little joke by making them come off. Had you not withheld from the press the information about the chocolates no doubt Diana would have read about it and put two and two together. Did you tell her they had been found, and where?'

Gaskin shook his head. 'No. Not yet. What's the use? The mischief has been done and there's no sense in making anyone else miserable. It'll have to be reported of course. Well, let's get home. I must say for an amateur you don't do too badly. What beats me is that a box of chocolates could kill anyone.'

'That box would come down with the force of a brick. You'd be surprised. Hit on the head it would have killed a horse, never mind a child without a hat. I once saw an airman killed by a spent cartridge, weighing perhaps an ounce, that fell from an aircraft flying at under a thousand feet. It went through a sun helmet like a bullet and then into his skull, knocking him out cold. Maybe that experience counted today. If so, you've had the benefit of it. Now, as you say, let's get along. As you've nothing on your mind we might stop for a snack on the way.'

Chapter 7

THE CASE OF THE AMATEUR YACHTSMEN

The tenuous blanket of dawn mist which night had spread over that part of the Atlantic known as the Western Approaches writhed and coiled as it was pierced by the lances of a new-born summer sun. It lifted, dispersing as it rose, so that in a few minutes it had vanished as completely as if it had never been, to reveal the broad face of the ocean in its most tranquil mood.

Air Police Constable 'Ginger' Hebblethwaite, flying at 5,000 feet, was glad to see it go, for he was bored with gazing into the empty blue void over his head or an apparently endless mass of cotton-wool below. He could now get on with his work, which on this occasion was not an ordinary routine patrol. He was looking for something, although he did not know exactly what it might be, except that it would come within the broad definition of transport, marine or air. Land, being little more than irregular smudges on the northern and southern horizons, could obviously be ruled out.

He checked his position, and finding himself beyond the end of his allotted beat, and a little concerned at being so far from solid ground in a machine with wheels on its undercarriage, he turned about to retrace his track, at the same time exploring the atmosphere for Biggles, who was – or should be – further west in the flying-boat amphibian 'Gadfly'. Failing to spot him, turning in wide circles but always edging nearer to the

English coast, he gave his attention to the sea.

This, to survey it thoroughly, would, he knew, be a longer operation, for strange though it may seem to a landsman who sees ships only from ground level, a vessel on the ocean, unless it happens to be a very big one, from a high altitude appears as a very small object indeed, easily overlooked. Moreover, although there are a great many ships in the world, of one sort or another, water covers so much of the earth's surface that when they are distributed there can be great distances between them. Although the English Channel is one of the busiest sea-traffic lanes, one can sail across it without seeing another ship.

On this occasion Ginger was not interested in big ships.

He made out a tanker, easily recognisable by the length of its hull with the superstructure aft, evidently from its course making for that base for such vessels, Falmouth Harbour. A big liner, outward bound, was hull down on the western horizon. Looking eastward he saw three warships coming down the middle of the Channel. Judging from the trails of white water they left behind them they were travelling at a rate of knots, presumably engaged in an exercise. There was little else: a few small craft, probably fishing-boats, were working closer inshore.

After another examination of the blue dome of heaven above and around him Ginger continued his search, methodically but without enthusiasm scanning the calm surface of the sea, section by section – without enthusiasm because he had been convinced from the outset that his assignment was in the nature of a wild-goose chase.

A tiny white feather which could only be foam caught his eye and held it. It was obviously the wake of a very small but high speed craft. Using his binoculars, which lay on the seat beside him ready for use, he was able to make out what he decided was a motor-boat, a cabin cruiser. It struck him as odd that such a boat, used chiefly for inshore pleasure trips, should be so far from land. Moreover, it was obviously going somewhere in a hurry. By watching the wake, which was constant, he was able to work out its approximate course. If it was maintained it would reach the English coast at Devon or Cornwall. A line extending behind it showed that it had started from a point in north-western France.

Ginger now took more interest. Was this what he was looking for? It was possible, if improbable. Easing the control column forward, he went 'downhill' for a closer inspection.

In doing this he presently saw something else, a dark object he had not previously noticed, either because it was small or more likely because it appeared not to be moving. He took it to be a fishing-boat. It had a mast, but the sail was furled. It was a mile or more from the motor-boat, but it lay directly on its course. He was sure the man at the wheel of the powered craft must have seen it, but so far he had made no move to change direction.

Ginger didn't know much about sea-fishing, but he was under the impression that small fishing craft kept on the move in order to work their nets. Could this be a rendezvous? Now having something to engage his interest he watched, half turning away, on half throttle both to lose a little more altitude and reduce engine noise.

Which brings us to the operation on which he was engaged. There was really nothing extraordinary about it; and, strictly speaking, it was not a matter for the British Air Police beyond co-operation in general terms between members of Interpol – The International Police Bureau. A robbery had occurred in France. A van carrying gold ingots to the value of nearly £100,000 had disappeared in transit between Paris and the port of Cherbourg. The van had been found abandoned. The gold had disappeared. So, of course, had the bandits. There was no clue. The French police thought it likely that an attempt would be made to smuggle the gold out of the country, wherefore sea and airports had been alerted, even though it seemed unlikely that the thieves would risk using any form of regular transport.

It seemed reasonable to suppose that if the gold left France it would be by a private conveyance, by sea or by air. To prevent this the forces of Interpol had been mustered, and to the British Air Police was given the assignment of watching the English Channel, both the sea and the air above it, for movements of a suspicious nature.

Biggles had accepted the task without pleasure, taking the view – as he told his Chief – that as the raid had been so cleverly planned it could be assumed that the disposal of the gold would be handled with the same efficiency. However, a watch had been laid on with all the police aircraft available, the pilots, generally flying solo, covering allotted sections of the Channel from dawn until dusk. Nothing could be done by aircraft after dark. On the present occasion it had been Ginger's turn, in an Auster, to watch for any sort of craft moving without any apparent reason between north-west

France and the Devon–Cornwall peninsular.

His interest in the motor-boat will now be understood. It had come from France. Where was it going? He also kept an eye on his petrol gauge, noting how much longer he would be able to remain airborne without refuelling.

His interest mounted when he saw the motor-boat run alongside the other craft – fishing-boat or whatever it might be – and stop. For what purpose. What could they have in common, he wondered? Such behaviour was at least unusual, if not suspicious. He kept his distance, watching, unable to see what was going on, yet not daring to go closer for fear those below might realise what he was doing.

The situation revealed the one big disadvantage under which an aircraft must work – as opposed, for instance, to a motor-car. A police officer in a car can challenge a suspected vehicle and if necessary search it. A police pilot in an aircraft can only watch. He cannot make direct contact, so he cannot ask questions. Thus it was with Ginger now.

The two craft lay side by side for perhaps ten minutes, ample time, Ginger reasoned, for something or someone to be transferred from one to the other. Then they parted; the motor-boat headed back for the long dark smudge that was the coast of France, the other setting a sail and taking up a course a little west of north. Extending an imaginary line, should this course be maintained, Ginger reckoned its landfall would be either Devon or Cornwall. As he couldn't track both craft he devoted his attention to the one making for England.

He was now getting worried about petrol. It was

obvious from the speed at which the fishing-boat was travelling, and the distance it had to go, that he would have to break off his patrol long before it reached land. There were other problems to exercise his mind. He realised that if he did follow his quarry to port, wherever that might be, he would probably lose sight of it among others of its class. Even from ground level he would be unable to identify it.

Yet he felt certain that he had seen some irregular transaction take place, probably nothing to do with the gold which was the primary object of his mission. That was too much to expect. The more he thought about it the more convinced he became that this meeting at sea was not an accident. The way it had happened suggested a prearrangement, an appointment. If this was correct there must have been an object. He could think of only one. Something, or perhaps somebody, had been switched from one boat to the other; but the way that object was now travelling, towards France or to England, he did not know and had no means of finding out. Why go to all this trouble unless the operation was illegal?

A detail about which he was in ignorance was the procedure that would be followed when the boat he was watching reached port. Would it automatically be checked by Customs and Excise officers? Was this a usual practice? He didn't know. In this case the officials could hardly know where the boat had been and would have no knowledge of the meeting that had taken place at sea. Even if he found a way of warning them, how was the boat to be identified?

While these thoughts had been passing through his mind Ginger had been cruising towards the English coast, clear in the bright sunlight. Now, suddenly he made up his mind to do two things. First he must be able to recognise his quarry if he saw it again. He wouldn't be likely to learn its name, but there might be some mark, some peculiarity, if only the colour of the sail, to make identification possible. If he succeeded in this he would make flat out for the nearest station where petrol was available, refuel and return, in time, he hoped, to watch the boat make port. There was a risk of losing it, but that had to be accepted.

Forthwith he set about putting the first part of his scheme into action. He went off for some distance, losing height, and then swung round in a wide circle on a course towards the coast, passing from a fairly low altitude the boat he was watching. Using his binoculars he was able to make out a common brown sail, and on it two letters in white, one above the other. They were N and K. There appeared to be a number under them, but it was too small for him to read. He also noted a small pointed pennant at the masthead. There was a device on it, but he could not make out what it was. A pile of dark-coloured objects lay on the deck. They could have been anything.

Having done as well as he expected, he flew straight on at top speed now making for the nearest RAF station, a training unit at Lidcombe, in south-west Devon. In ten minutes he was there.

Having landed and reported to Station Headquarters, the production of his police pass and Interpol Carnet were sufficient to obtain the service he needed. While this was being attended to, having permission to use the telephone, he put through a call to Algy, who was on duty in the office at Scotland Yard, and reported the incident of the meeting of the two craft at sea. He asked for Biggles to be told. He also suggested it might be worth while letting the coastguard service know about it as they might be interested.

In a few minutes he had signed for the petrol and oil he had taken and was on his way back to the coast.

Reaching the open sea, he made for the last known position of the boat in which he was interested, expecting to find it on the same course and closer to land. To his chagrin it was not where it should have been. In fact, it was not even in sight. Knowing it could not be far away, he made a systematic search, and after a little while found it lying inconspicuously, close inshore, against a rocky headland; which explained why he had had some difficulty in spotting it. He noted that it must have moved faster than he had thought possible. The sail was down, which also surprised him considering its position, and he could only conclude that it had an engine of some sort. He could see two men moving about on deck, but it took him a little while to make out what they were doing.

It was a line of black dots on the water that eventually told him. He had seen lobster pots before – or rather the cork buoys that marked the position of the wickerwork traps that had been lowered to the sea bed. He realised that what he had seen lying on deck was a heap of lobster pots.

On the face of it nothing could be more natural, and as Ginger flew on he had a feeling that he had been making a mountain out of a molehill. He had to consult the Admiralty chart he carried in order to learn the name of the short, stumpy, rocky headland, against which the boat was working – if in fact it had a name, since it was hardly large enough to be called a cape. He made it out to be Bull Head, an insignificant physical feature apparently shown only on large-scale maps, for he had never heard of it.

Still flying straight on he had second thoughts about the situation. Why, if the boat was a lobster fisher, had it wasted time far out over the deep water of the Channel? There seemed to be something peculiar about that. However, there was nothing more he could do at the moment. Having plenty of petrol, he resolved to check where the suspect eventually came to anchor or found a mooring. So, from a safe distance, he watched the boat, under sail, cruise along the coast for two or three miles and then turn into the little harbour of Poltruan, where he lost sight of it among the small craft already there.

As there was nothing more he could do, still full of doubts about the whole business, he set a course for home. The time was still only nine o'clock.

It was some minutes short of noon when he walked into the office at Scotland Yard to find Biggles and Bertie there, both having come in for food and a rest after four hours in the air. Algy had departed to continue the patrol.

'Well, did you see anything exciting at your end?' greeted Biggles.

'I wouldn't say exciting, but maybe interesting,' returned Ginger, dropping into a chair. 'There may be nothing to it, in which case all I've done is waste a lot of time and petrol. I rang Algy when I went ashore to refuel. Didn't he leave a note about it?'

'He did. Now you're here you can give us the details.'

'Did Algy ring the coastguard people as I suggested?'

'Yes, he did that, but as they haven't reported back, either they did nothing about it or, if they did, drew blank.'

Ginger shrugged. 'There was nothing else I could do. This is what happened.' He went on to describe his activities of the morning.

When he had finished Biggles said: 'I don't see how you could have done more. Queer business. You did right to report it. This meeting at sea, obviously an appointment, looks suspicious, to say the least of it. Something irregular was cooking, that's certain.'

Bertie spoke: 'Why should a boat from our side go so far afield if its real intention was to bag a few lobsters?'

'That's what I asked myself,' answered Ginger.

'Well, you did as much as you could,' consoled Biggles. 'If the Excise people aren't interested I don't see why we should lose any sleep over it.'

The intercom telephone at his elbow buzzed. He picked up the receiver. 'Bigglesworth here.' Then he listened for two or three minutes, a wry smile creeping over his face. At the finish all he said was: 'Very well, sir.' He replaced the instrument and looked up. 'That's all the thanks you get for trying to be helpful,' he remarked bitterly.

'I imagine that was the Chief,' guessed Ginger.

Biggles nodded. 'It seems I spoke a bit too soon. Some senior coastguard official has just rung up the Air Commodore to request that in future the Air Police mind their own business.'

'Here, I say, that's a bit thick,' exclaimed Bertie indignantly. 'What exactly are we to take that to mean?'

'When Ginger's boat returned to harbour at Poltruan

some officers were there waiting for it. They made a thorough search.'

'What did they find?'

'A fish box.'

Ginger half rose in his chair. 'Ah! What was in it?'

'Fish,' answered Biggles succinctly.

Bertie threw back his head and laughed.

Ginger scowled. 'What's so funny about that?'

'Your expression. Sorry, dear boy.'

Biggles was not amused. 'The two chaps on board admitted they'd been out in the Channel for a sail, the weather being perfect. They'd tried hand-lining for fish, but all they'd managed to catch were a few pollack. They'd seen nothing of a motor-boat.'

'That makes them liars for a start,' growled Ginger. 'I saw a powered craft tie up alongside. That's why I kept an eye on them. You don't suppose I imagined it.'

'I'm sure you didn't.'

'Was nothing said about lobsters?'

'Not as far as I know. If you'll listen I'll tell you the rest of the information the Air Commodore has just passed on to me. The boat, which by the way has an auxiliary engine, doesn't belong to a local fisherman. Actually it's a small Dutch barge that has been converted into a private yacht. It's owned by a couple of London gents – whatever that may mean – keen amateur yachtsmen who are taking a holiday sailing along the south coast. They've been at Poltruan for a week. According to them they're members of a well-known yacht club, for which reason they took exception to being questioned. They demanded an apology and, I'm sorry to say, got one.'

'Well, blow me down!' breathed Bertie.

Biggles went on. 'I don't care who they are. What I don't like is the way we've been given the brush-off as if we were a bunch of interfering twits. That's the thanks you get for trying to be efficient.'

'What had the Chief to say about it?'

'He said we should be more careful.'

'I call that pretty rich,' muttered Ginger.

'Forget it. He's probably feeling a bit sore at having been ticked off.'

'I feel more than a *bit* sore,' asserted Ginger.

'I don't take it too kindly myself,' put in Bertie, polishing his monocle briskly. 'It would give me lots of joy if we could prove some of these johnnies were wrong and we were right.'

'And me,' agreed Biggles thoughtfully. 'That isn't impossible, either. From the fact that these so-called gents lied about the motor-boat it wouldn't surprise me if, when the Customs men went aboard, they adopted a high and mighty attitude as their best defence. Crooks can be pretty slick at that sort of thing.'

'Then in spite of what has been said you still think they have been up to something?' said Ginger.

'I think what they did this morning justifies a more convincing explanation than the one they gave. If they've put down lobster pots round Bull Head it means they'll be going back there, either tonight or tomorrow morning. I've a good mind to run down and have a look at these amateur yachtsmen.'

'Why not, old boy?' said Bertie, briskly. 'It can do no harm.'

Biggles glanced at the clock. 'To be mobile when we get there we shall need a car, which means going down by road. It's about a five-hour run and will mean staying the night. No matter. Let's press on.'

In ten minutes, with the emergency cases of small kit held in readiness for urgent occasions, they were on their way to Poltruan.

They arrived at the little Cornish port just after seven, having stopped for a meal on the way, to find its narrow streets crowded with trippers and holiday-makers. This was to be expected for it was the high season, and they would have struck the same conditions at any seaside town, large or small. Having with some difficulty found a place to park the car, they made their way to the harbour, a simple affair formed by a concrete mole thrown at an angle half-way across a tiny natural bay.

Reaching the sea, Ginger indicated a towering mass of rock further along the deeply indented coast. 'That's Bull Head,' he remarked. 'The place I told you about. The lobster pots were put down on the far side.'

'We may have a closer look at it soon,' said Biggles.

Poltruan, like most West Country coastal villages – for it was little more than that – had until modern times been for centuries the home of a few families which for generations, father and son, had made a precarious livelihood by fishing. There were still half a dozen well-worn Cornish-built fishing-boats in the harbour, but much of the space was now occupied by pleasure craft, privately owned small yachts, but mostly dinghies of various sizes, with outboard motors, which could be hired with or without a local man in charge. Fishing for mackerel with hand-lines was popular, these fish occurring in large numbers and being easy to catch. A party was just coming ashore with a good basket.

Said Biggles, as they stopped on the quay to survey

the scene: 'There's the boat we came to look at, moored inside the mole. Let's move nearer.'

Joining the several casual visitors who were doing the same thing, they strolled along the concrete barrier, looking at the various craft that lay alongside, until they came to the one in which they had a particular interest, identified by the burgee, or pennant, that decorated the masthead. There was not much to see. The boat itself was not, strictly speaking, a fisher; it was one of the type known as a Dutch 'barge', of shallow draught and built of massive timbers to stand up to the battering of the North Sea, which can on occasion be nasty. It had obviously been converted into a yacht, which many had been on account of their seaworthy qualities. Its name was *Scamperer*.

The chief objects of interest were the two men – presumably the so-called 'gents' – who lounged, smoking pipes, by the companion-way. Both were of early middle age and dressed for the part; polo-necked jerseys, linen slacks and rope-soled canvas shoes. They took no notice of the spectators. Nor for that matter did spectators take much notice of them. The spectacle, such as it was, was commonplace.

'Let's see if we can find out anything about them,' said Biggles, leading the way back to the wharf.

There was not much activity at this hour. Two men were moving some empty fish boxes into one of the wooden buildings behind. Others, who had brought their nets ashore, were talking as they cleaned them and made them into neat piles. An old greybeard wearing the usual fisherman's kit sat alone on a bollard watching a scene he must have witnessed thousands of times.

Biggles stopped by him. 'Nice day,' he observed.

The old man agreed.

'You must have seen a lot of changes,' prompted Biggles, to open a conversation.

The old man, like most of his type, was willing to talk. 'Yes,' he grunted, 'and none of 'em for the better.'

'Do you get many lobsters around here?'

'A few, when the water's right. Mostly small nowadays. They've been fished too hard. These youngsters keep 'em all, large and small. So do some of the visitors, who don't seem to realise they're doing the local people out of their living. I'm always saying, if this goes on there soon won't be any lobsters.'

Biggles changed the subject. Pointing, he asked: 'Is that what you call Bull Head?'

'Yes, that's Bull Head.'

'I'd have thought that was a good place to pick up a few lobsters.'

'No better than anywhere else. It's a dangerous place.'

'In what way?'

'A lot o' gulls nest there. Kids were always falling and breaking their bones trying to get to the eggs. Now the top has been fenced off and a notice put up telling people to keep clear. The caves are dangerous, too.'

'Caves?'

'Full o' caves. The Head is a honeycomb. Some get flooded at high tide. People have got cut off and drowned there in my time, trying to find the old smugglers' way through the Head. There's always been a tale it's possible to get right through the Head from one side to the other, but I've never heard of anyone doing it. This is the time o' day people get trapped; low tide and on the turn. When she comes back she comes in

125

too fast for people to get out.'

Again Biggles changed the subject. 'What's that old Dutch barge doing here?'

'Just put in to lay off for a bit, I suppose. It's been here for a week. Goes for a cruise when there's a breeze. It was here last year about the same time. They're good boats. They tell me more and more of 'em are being fitted out as yachts.'

'Who told you?'

'Mr Trelawny. He's one of the owners of *Scamperer*. His partner's name is Pennington. Nice chaps. They've often had a word with me.'

'Trelawny. That name is as Cornish as they make 'em.'

'Mr Trelawny – that's him, with the fair hair – tells me his family lived near here. He was born here.'

'Which means he knows all about the place.'

'He talks like he does. Are you gentlemen staying here?'

'We thought of it, if we can find a lodging.'

'You'll have a job. The place is packed out. Hardly room to move. That's what it's got like. I dunno what things are coming to. Still, there's more money in this tourist business than ever there was in fishing.'

Biggles paused. 'What are the chances of hiring a boat?'

'No trouble about that.'

'I can handle a boat, so I don't need anyone with me. I'd like one with a motor.'

The old man pointed with the stem of his pipe. 'There's the *Puffin* just in. She's had a party out fishing. A nice roomy little craft with a fixed engine. She ought to suit you. Go and speak with Harry Trevethin. That's him, helping the people ashore.'

'Thanks. I'll go and see if I can get her.'

As Biggles walked along to the boat, which some obvious tourists were leaving, he said quietly to Ginger: 'Slip back to the car and fetch the torch. It's in the front panel – or should be.'

Ginger turned away.

Biggles spoke to the owner of the boat. 'May I and my friends hire her for a trip?'

'When do you want her?'

'Now. The old chap sitting over there recommended her.'

'How long do you want her for?'

'An hour or two maybe. Say a run along the coast past Bull Head and back.'

The man glanced round the sky. 'It's getting a bit late.' The sun was, in fact, well down. 'Do you want me to go with you?'

'No. We can manage. We've had plenty of experience with boats.'

'I don't like her being out after dark.'

'We shan't be late. You needn't worry about us. There's a full moon to make things easy if we're not back by nightfall, although I expect we shall be.'

The man considered Biggles with speculative eyes. 'You look all right.'

Biggles looked puzzled. 'All right for what?'

'Some youngsters nowadays think it's smart to hire a boat and leave it miles away to get out of paying for it. Which also means I have to go and fetch it.'

'If that's the trouble I'll pay in advance.'

'Never mind. You look a responsible sort of chap. I reckon I can trust you. All right, then. I'll go and have my supper. You'll find me here when you get back.'

'Is she all right for oil?'

'Plenty. Get aboard. I'll see you off.'

By this time Ginger had returned. They all took their places, Biggles at the tiller, as the boatman started the engine for them. He climbed back ashore and the boat chugged its way out of the harbour to the open sea. As it passed the *Scamperer*, still at its mooring, the two men who owned her were still on deck. Another man had joined them. Once out of the harbour, on the far side of the mole, only the mainmast, with the distinguishing pennant hanging limply at the peak, could be seen.

Said Bertie: 'Would I be right in guessing that the purpose of this naval operation is to have a look at the caves of Bull Head?'

'You would. That's why I sent Ginger to fetch a torch. We wouldn't have got far without one.'

'You think we might find something there?' put in Ginger.

'It's possible.'

'Meaning the business of putting down lobster pots was a blind?'

'Could be, particularly as that old salt hinted that lobstering was now really a waste of time. He said something else that made me wonder. Trelawny, one of the two men, was born in these parts; which means he must know all about Bull Head and its caves. There may be nothing to it, but the *Scamperer*'s trip this morning, half-way across the Channel to meet a boat from France, smells fishy to me – apart from lobsters. If nothing comes of it, well, a sniff of sea air won't have done us any harm.'

The boat was now approaching the eastern face of

Bull Head with the sun setting behind it. It was actually a blunt-nosed cliff about a hundred feet high projecting fifty or sixty yards into the sea. What the old man had said about gulls was confirmed. Hundreds could be seen on the ledges, and others were drifting in from all directions presumably to roost for the night. A number of holes, mostly at water level, were apparently the caves to which the old man had referred.

The boat, with its steady *phut-phut-phut*, went on to the far side, revealing the width of the little promontory, a matter of perhaps no more than seventy to a hundred yards. Holes, where storm water had eaten into it, were frequent, some large, some small, no more than shallow depressions. There were one or two yawning caverns. On this side the cliff was not actually sheer; but it sloped back steeply and was no doubt the place where fool-hardy boys had risked their limbs for gulls' eggs. There was no beach. A landing could only be made on the rock.

'The lobster pots haven't been lifted yet, anyhow,' remarked Ginger as, having rounded the frowning buttress of rock, the cork marker floats came into view.

There were six of them, more or less in line, at frequent intervals near the foot of a cliff pitted with holes, into some of which the rising tide was already lapping.

'The question,' said Biggles as he took the boat close in, 'is how long the *Scamperer* is going to leave the pots here? I mean, how long will it be before it comes back for them? I'm thinking that if the men aboard are engaged in a racket of some sort, they must have had a shock when they returned to port and found Excise officers waiting for them. They must be wondering why.

Anyway, that should be enough to warn them to be extra careful; that their activities are under suspicion. In which case surely they'll think twice in future about taking contraband into Poltruan, if that's what they've been doing.'

'What beats me is why they dumped their cargo here, if in fact they did that,' said Ginger. 'It would almost seem as if they had an idea they might be checked when they got back to the harbour.'

'I don't see how that could happen unless an accomplice ashore spotted the Excise men, and guessing why they were there sent out a warning signal by radio. Or, of course, there's just a chance they might have suspected that the aircraft waffling about near them was watching them.'

'I kept a fair distance away,' stated Ginger. 'Still, I must admit they couldn't fail to see me.'

Bertie changed the subject. 'I say, old boy, exploring all these caves is going to be a long job.'

'They'll hardly need exploring. If the *Scamperer* landed anything here it shouldn't be far away. Moreover, I think it's safe to assume it would be in a cave above the high water mark, and there aren't so many of those. Some are already flooding.'

'We'd better keep clear of those,' requested Ginger seriously. 'Remember what the old man said about people getting trapped.'

'I'll watch it, don't worry. Let's get on. We've no time to lose. It'll be dark inside an hour. The best way to work would be for me to put you off at different caves for a quick look round for signs of a recent visit. I'll stay in the boat. I'm taking no chances of getting stranded here. We'll start at this end. If either of you need the torch I'll hand it over; but with the sun low on this side you should have enough light for as far as you're likely to go in.'

Nothing more was said. The task began in the manner Biggles had suggested.

Considering what they had to do, they covered the ground quickly. Most of the caves proved to be short. Some, however, ran deeply into the rock, further than they felt inclined to go, and according to Biggles' theory further than it was necessary to go. He still maintained that if anything had been hidden in a cave it should be just inside; so why risk losing their way by going further? The extent of one or two of the caves gave some support to the old tale that it was possible to go in one side of Bull Head and come out the other.

When at the end of half an hour all the caves had been investigated without result, they stood together at the entrance to a high, narrow cleft in the rock, the last to be explored. Ginger, taking the torch, had been in for some distance, although not to the far end. Like most caves it was a gloomy, depressing place, the atmosphere heavy with the smell of debris thrown in by waves at high water – pebbles, shells, seaweed and rotting pieces of wood. At the moment the rising water was still two or three feet below the entrance to the cave.

'It looks as if we've drawn blank,' said Biggles, holding the boat with the boat-hook so that the others could get on board. 'With the light going there isn't much more we can do. I'm surprised. I would have bet on finding evidence of the *Scamperer*'s crew having been here. After all, why did they come here if not to put something ashore?'

'Maybe they were serious about their lobster fishing,'

suggested Ginger moodily, nodding at the cork floats a few yards away. 'I wonder if they've caught anything?'

'Just a minute,' answered Biggles with a sudden change of voice. 'You've put a notion in my head.' He tossed his cigarette end overboard and, using the boat-hook against the rock, pushed, so that the boat drifted out to the nearest float. 'Let's see if they *have* caught anything. Haul up the pot, Bertie.'

Bertie felt down for the rope and, hand over hand, pulled the basketwork trap to the surface. It was empty. He smiled bleakly. 'Nothing doing,' he said, and was about to drop the contrivance back into the sea when Biggles stopped him.

'Hold hard! I'm not surprised there's nothing in it. There's no bait. I was under the impression that in order to induce the lobsters to commit suicide it was necessary to encourage them with a lump of meat, a dead fish, or something of that sort. There's something fishy about this in more senses than one. Why put down a trap without a bait?'

The boat was moved a few yards and the operation was repeated.

'There's something here all right,' declared Bertie, as he dragged up the trap. 'Feels like a bally octopus.' The basket came into sight. With some difficulty he lifted it inboard and dropped it with a thump.

Nobody spoke. All eyes were on the lobster pot.

The silence was broken by Biggles. 'By thunder!' he breathed. 'We *have* made a catch. You realise what this is?'

Ginger answered. 'Looks like a load of bricks.'

'Bricks is right. Gold bricks. This must be the stuff stolen in France.' Biggles moved with alacrity. 'Quick,' he said tersely. 'This isn't all of it. The rest must be in some of the others. Take the gold out and chuck the trap back overboard. Get cracking. If the *Scamperer* should roll up and catch us at this there'll be hell to pay. I'll handle the boat.'

In the fast-failing daylight the activity in the boat was now intense. Ten minutes and the work was done. Two more pots contained gold bars. The others were empty – except for a small crab.

'Okay. That must be the lot,' snapped Biggles, when the ingots lay in a heap on the floor of the boat.

'What are we going to do with it?' asked Ginger. 'We can't take this into Poltruan without the owner of the boat seeing it, and that's likely to cause a sensation.'

Biggles hesitated, staring at the gold. 'You're so right. When the men on the *Scamperer* heard about it, and that wouldn't take long, they'd either bolt or disclaim all knowledge of it. Either way it would come to the same thing. We couldn't prove they'd put it here. The gold isn't enough. We want them in the bag, too.'

'How are you going to manage that?'

'Leave the stuff here and grab them when they come back for it. We'll put it in the cave; bury it under some of the muck and nip back to Poltruan for help. There are at least three men in the gang. They may carry guns. If so, trying to arrest them with our bare hands in a place like this would be asking for trouble.'

'We should have brought guns,' said Bertie.

'Never mind what we *should* have done. Who could have guessed things would turn out like this? Let's get on shifting the stuff. The *Scamperer* may come round the Head at any moment.'

A quarter of an hour of feverish activity saw the gold

thrown into a depression a little way inside the cave and there covered with seaweed and any other rubbish that came to hand. By the time the job was done the tide was within inches of the lip of the cave.

'Now let's get back to Poltruan,' ordered Biggles, holding the boat close in.

Ginger raised a hand. 'Listen. I can hear something.'

'Water dripping.'

'Sounds like voices.'

Biggles peered into the dusk towards the end of the cliff. 'No one here.'

An instant later came a curious hollow echo. It was, without doubt, a human voice.

'Here, I say, old boy,' muttered Bertie in a low tense voice. 'The blighters are coming this way, through the cave from the far side.'

'Trelawny, the man who was born here, should know the way,' put in Ginger.

'They must be coming for the gold,' stated Biggles. 'We'd better get out.'

This brief conversation had been carried on in a whisper. Meanwhile, voices were coming nearer, making it evident there were at least two men. Ginger had moved to step into the boat when Biggles said sharply: 'Wait! The *Scamperer* is just coming round the Head. I wondered how they intended getting to the pots without a boat. Looks like we're the meat in a sandwich. This means trouble.' He looked up the backward sloping face of the cliff. 'Ginger, do you think you could get that way to the top?'

'I'll have a shot at it.'

'Then get going. Make for the road. Stop any car for a lift. Get to a phone and call the Yard. Explain the

134

position. Say we need help, urgently. We'll hang on as long as we can. Careful how you go.'

Without another word Ginger set off on his hazardous climb. A dim twilight still lingered.

Bertie joined Biggles in the boat just as two men appeared at the mouth of the cave. One was Trelawny. He carried a torch. The other was a stranger. Little could be seen of his face by reason of a dark beard. Both men wore polo-necked sweaters and gum boots. They had been talking in a casual way, but stopped abruptly when they saw the boat. They advanced slowly.

'What the hell are you doing here?' asked Trelawny, in an astonished voice.

'We've been admiring the sunset,' returned Biggles evenly.

The other man spoke, apparently annoyed to find them there. 'Thinking of buying it?' he sneered.

'Why, were you thinking of selling it?'

At this juncture the *Scamperer* came up. Nosing its way in, it stopped. There were two men on board, Pennington and another stranger. 'What's going on here?' enquired Pennington curtly.

'You tell me,' invited Biggles. 'I had no idea the place was so popular.'

A long, uncomfortable pause. Then Pennington, frowning, went on: 'Have you been interfering with our lobster pots?'

'What would I do with raw lobsters? I like my lobsters cooked.'

'How long are you staying here?'

'I hadn't thought about it. Never mind us. We shan't get in your way.'

A piece of rock came clattering down from above to

fall with a splash in the water.

This, naturally, caused everyone to look up; but it was too dark for anything to be seen.

'What was that?' asked Trelawny, looking at Biggles. 'Is somebody up there?'

'Yes. A friend of mine.'

'What the devil's he doing?'

'Taking a short cut home. He had some urgent business to attend to. We were in no hurry.'

The four men, two on the boat, two standing at the lip of the cavern into which water was now trickling, looked at each other. Their predicament was obvious. They couldn't proceed in front of witnesses with what they had come to do; nor could they for the same reason discuss openly a situation for which they must have been unprepared. As for Biggles, he was simply playing for time; to give Ginger as long as possible to do what was required of him. At this stage Biggles and Bertie might perhaps have gone. In fact, this would probably have suited the gold thieves, who could then have got on with their business – until they discovered the gold had gone, which would not have taken more than a minute. Then anything might have happened. Wherefore Biggles pursued his delaying tactics.

'I take it these are your lobster pots,' he resumed.

'They are.'

'I suppose you know the local people take a poor view of tourists' butting in on what they regard as their private preserves?'

'I couldn't care less what they think,' growled Pennington.

'After all, it's their livelihood,' Biggles pointed out, wondering how far Ginger had got. At least he hadn't fallen.

'So what? Sea-fishing is free for all.'

Biggles shrugged. 'I'm not disputing that. Have it your own way.'

It looked as if this futile conversation might go on for some time; but it seemed that Pennington became suddenly impatient, or suspicious, for he moved his boat to the nearest lobster float, which happened to be one of those that had contained some of the gold bars. He reached down to the float.

'This is where the balloon goes up,' breathed Bertie in Biggles' ear.

Pennington pulled on the rope. Took the strain. Lifted. His expression changed abruptly as the weight told him the truth. He looked up. 'There's nothing here,' he said, in a thin tense voice. He did not say what he expected to find.

'Are you sure it's the right one?' said Trelawny, from the cave. 'Try another.'

Pennington tested the next pot. He didn't bother to pull it up. The weight must have told him all he needed to know. 'Empty,' he rasped.

This information was received with a shocked silence. It lasted for the best part of a minute, the men looking at each other as if uncertain about what to do next. Then Pennington, without haste, took an automatic from his pocket and pointed it at Biggles. 'Come on. What have you done with it?' he grated, tight-lipped.

Biggles affected surprised innocence. 'What's all this about? Done with what? How many lobsters did you expect to find?'

'You know what I'm talking about.'

'How should I?'

'Don't give me that! You poached our pots and took what you found in 'em.'

The atmosphere was now taut.

Biggles, still playing for time, continued to pretend ignorance. 'You're making a hell of a fuss over a few perishing lobsters. If you think we pinched 'em you're wrong. You're welcome to all the lobsters, crabs, or any other fish you can find in this boat. Look for yourself if you don't believe me; but don't be too long about it. It's time I was taking the boat back.'

Pennington didn't answer. He brought the *Scamperer* alongside the *Puffin* and, gun in hand, jumped aboard. He searched, examining the locker, turning over the cushions and odd gear. Of course he did not find what he was looking for. 'It isn't here,' he informed his associates.

'It must be somewhere handy,' declared Trelawny.

'What have you done with it?' demanded Pennington harshly, glaring at Biggles.

To which Biggles replied, calmly: 'If you'll tell me what you're looking for I might be able to help you. I thought it was lobsters you were after.'

In his frustration Pennington looked ready to commit murder. 'No, it wasn't lobsters.'

'Then what was it?'

'You know damn well what it was. Gold.'

Biggles smiled broadly. 'Gold! In lobster pots? Is this some kind of a game? Treasure island stuff? You've come to the wrong place. You should try the Caribbean.'

In an atmosphere that was now explosive Bertie chipped in. 'I remember when I was a kid. . .'

'Shut up,' snapped Trelawny. He looked at the faces of his companions. 'Well, what are we going to do?'

Biggles answered. 'You can do what you like, but I'm going home. The chap at Poltruan from whom we hired this boat is likely to raise an alarm, supposing we're in trouble.'

Deep dusk had in fact dimmed the scene. Ginger had been gone a good half-hour, and as nothing had been seen or heard of him he had presumably got away. The position was unchanged, Trelawny and one man standing at the mouth of the cave, the water level at their feet, the two boats touching with engines silent, rocking slightly in a gentle swell.

'You're not going anywhere till you tell us what you've done with it,' swore Pennington, venomously.

'Maybe someone put it in the cave,' suggested Biggles, hopefully.

'That's an idea. We'll soon settle that.' Pennington and his companion jumped ashore to join the others.

Biggles was amazed. This of course was what he wanted, but he could hardly believe his ruse to get them all ashore had worked so easily. He could only suppose that anxiety had made them careless. Or it may have been they had been deceived by his inconsequential manner. However that may be, in the light of the torch they began looking about them for the lost treasure.

To appreciate what followed, the position of the two boats must be explained. The *Puffin*, being first on the spot, was lying almost flush with the entrance to the cave. The *Scamperer*, almost touching her on the seaward side, was practically holding her there. This was probably accidental rather than deliberate, since there had been no hostilities when these positions were taken up.

Biggles caught Bertie's eye. He winked a warning to

stand by. Then, very quietly he picked up the boat-hook and pushed it hard against the face of the rock. The *Puffin* moved out, slowly, taking her heavier consort with her. A yard of water appeared between the *Puffin* and the cave. Biggles rose and put all his weight on the pole. The distance widened to two yards ... three. Biggles' eyes never left the dark figures in the cave, silhouetted in the light of the torch. He murmured to Bertie: 'Be ready to duck.' He was no longer able to reach the cliff with the boat-hook, but the way on the boats had taken them out to five or six yards when the end came.

Trelawny, happening to look round, realised what Biggles had done. He let out a cry of alarm. 'Here, you, come back,' he shouted.

Biggles' answer was to hand the boat-hook to Bertie with a crisp: 'Hang on to the yacht and crank the *Puffin*'s engine.' As it came to life, and the propeller churned the water into foam, Trelawny, seeing what was intended, took a desperate chance. He jumped for the stern of the *Puffin* as it moved slowly away. He fell short. There was a mighty splash. When he came up he still struggled to reach the *Puffin*; but when Bertie pointed the boat-hook at him he changed his mind and made back for the cave. In gum boots and woollen clothes it took him all his time to reach it. His friends dragged him in.

'Now for the fireworks,' said Biggles, jockeying the two boats further away.

Hardly had he said the words than a gun flashed. Nothing else could be seen. There was no torch. Trelawny, who had been holding it, had apparently dropped it in the sea. More shots were fired, although what the bandits hoped to achieve by this was not clear, since killing or wounding the men handling the boats would have served no useful purpose. Perhaps they didn't think of this. Perhaps they hoped to frighten them into returning.

The boats made a target too big to miss, and several shots struck them. Splinters flew. No harm was done. Biggles, working the tiller, was flat on the floor. So was Bertie, still hanging on to the boat-hook, the business end of which was still engaged with the *Scamperer's* bowsprit. The distance between the boats and the land increased. The shooting stopped. From the direction of the cave came sounds of a furious argument.

'Jolly good,' remarked Bertie cheerfully. 'That's queered their bally pitch. What next, old boy?'

'You get on the *Scamperer* and throw me a line. I'll make fast and tow her away with us. Watch how you go. We're still in range.'

This was done, while ashore threats turned to pleadings for rescue as the water was rising in the cave.

'We can't leave 'em to drown,' said Bertie with some concern when he returned to the *Puffin*.

'They won't drown, don't worry,' replied Biggles. 'They may get their feet wet, that's all. The high-water mark in the cave is never more than a couple of feet up the wall. Having got them where we want them, we'll leave them there for a bit to cool off. Trelawny, if he knows his way about, may get them to higher ground inside the caves, although if he's lost his torch that won't be easy. We'll tow the yacht round the Head to see if there's anything coming this way. Ginger should have done something by this time.'

When the *Puffin* turned the end of the cliff it was clear

that something was happening. A cutter, showing lights and travelling fast, was coming towards them. When it was within hailing distance a stern voice ordered them to stop.

Biggles cut his engine. 'Police here,' he called.

The cutter drew alongside. Aboard were several men, police and coastguards in uniform, others in plain clothes.

'What's happened?' questioned a uniformed inspector.

Biggles explained in as few words as possible. He described the cave in which the crooks had been marooned.

'I know the one,' stated a coastguard. 'The only way they could get out would be by going back through the Head to where some of 'em got in. It'd be a tricky business with the water at this level.'

'They haven't a torch. I think they lost it in the sea.'

'Then they'd be mad to move. They're safe where they are, but further in there are places where high water comes up to the roof. I know. I was once nearly caught that way.'

'Still, to be sure we ought to cover both sides of the Head,' decided the inspector. 'But we can't do that with only one boat.'

'Take this one. We don't want it.' Biggles indicated the *Scamperer*.

'That's an idea. How many are there of 'em, did you say?'

'Four. Some, if not all, carry guns.'

'If I know anything they'll be glad to see us,' asserted an old coastguard. 'Those caves are no joke at high water after dark.'

Said the inspector to Biggles: 'You coming back with us?'

'Not unless you want me to. I'll leave the rest to you. You'll find the gold about ten yards in, on the left. We ought to get back to Poltruan. Mr Trevethin will be getting worried about his boat.'

'All right, then. We'll see you later.'

Two men from the cutter went aboard the *Scamperer* and took over. Biggles cast off and the *Puffin* chugged on its way towards the harbour lights of Poltruan.

Waiting for them was not only the owner of the boat, but Ginger, who said he'd only just got there. 'Everything all right?' he enquired. 'I missed the boat.'

'All finished and buttoned up,' reported Biggles. 'When I've settled with Mr Trevethin for his boat I'll tell you about it.'

That really concludes the case of the amateur yachtsmen who, it was revealed subsequently, were originally just that and nothing more; but having engaged in a little quiet smuggling on their own account, they became involved with an international gang who operated on a more ambitious scale. It was the old story of petty pilfering leading to serious crime.

The affair of the stolen gold needs little explanation. Having got away with it in France, the crooks wanted it out of the country as quickly as possible. England would do as well as anywhere. Trelawny and Pennington were available with their yacht, so shipment seemed an easy matter. And so no doubt it would have been were it not for eyes watching the Channel from above. Trelawny's defence was that he and his partner had been blackmailed into doing what they had done; but, as was pointed out by the prosecution, this, if true, would not have been possible had they not already broken the law.

Why was the gold taken to the caves? The answer is interesting. It turned out that in spite of Ginger's care to keep well away from the yacht, Trelawny had become suspicious of an aircraft circling in the vicinity for so long and thought it safer not to sail straight into Poltruan for fear of what we know did actually happen. Excise men were waiting. He had known about the caves from boyhood. The lobster pots on board had been used on previous occasions as a cover for contraband. They were now used for the gold, which it was supposed could be picked up later when the coast was clear – literally.

Of the four men who came to collect it under cover of darkness, two were members of the big gang. They had been waiting at Poltruan for the *Scamperer* to come in with the gold on board. From the two yachtsmen they learned where the gold had been hidden, and why. Not trusting each other overmuch, they had gone to fetch it in two parties, one by sea and the other through the caves, in this way keeping Trelawny and Pennington apart in case they contemplated a double-cross.

Actually, their scheme had come unstuck largely through this distrust and the impatience of the gold bandits to recover their loot; and, of course, they reckoned without the Air Police who, incidentally, were given full credit for the way they had handled the affair.

It only remains to be said that all four men received long terms of imprisonment. The *Scamperer* was confiscated, and the gold returned to its rightful owners.

Chapter 8

THE BOY WHO WATCHED THE PLANES GO BY

Biggles sat at his desk, a little smile on his face as he perused three pieces of paper, pinned together, which had just been delivered from the head office.

'Something funny?' queried Ginger, happening to look up from where he was working.

'Not really.'

'Then why laugh?'

'I'm not laughing, although I must admit to some amusement at the way the writer of this letter, apparently a budding detective, expresses himself. Straight to the point. No words wasted.'

'What's worrying him?'

'He doesn't say; but he must have something on his mind or he wouldn't have gone to the trouble of writing this letter and spending threepence of his pocket-money on a stamp. The Chief has sent it up with a covering note asking us to look into it if we think it worth while. Here, read it for yourself. Note the address on the envelope.'

Ginger took the papers and he, too, smiled as he read aloud: ' "*Air Detective Bigglesworth, Scotland Yard, London.*" ' Turning to the letter, he continued: ' "*Dear Biggles, I have read about the things you do and I reckon something is going on here you ought to know about. Yours respectfully, Robin Stone. Aged thirteen.*" '

Ginger tossed the papers back on the desk. 'I wouldn't waste much time on that.'

'You wouldn't?'

'No.'

'Why not?'

'It can't amount to anything. What could a kid of that age know?'

'The answer might surprise you. It's time you caught up with the new generation. The modern boy goes about with his eyes and ears wide open – and there's plenty for him to see and hear that didn't arise when we were his age. We don't know what this lad may have seen, but he has obviously spotted something to make him suspicious or he wouldn't have made the effort to write this letter. At his age one doesn't write letters for the fun of it, particularly as they cost money to post. This boy has done what he thinks is the right thing to do. If he's prepared to go to that trouble and expense it would be a poor return to throw the letter in the waste-paper basket.'

Ginger nodded. 'I see what you mean. Pity he didn't say in his letter what it was all about.'

'There could be reasons for that. In the first place it might be a long story, too involved for him to put down in writing. It might not sound very convincing, and a boy thinks twice before perhaps making a fool of himself. This one is a country lad. You see where he writes from. Marsh Cottage, Shingleton, Suffolk. I've never heard of the place. Must be a village, in which case we may suppose Robin goes to the village school.'

'All right. What are you going to do about it?'

'Unless we ignore the letter, and I shall certainly not do that, there's only one thing we can do. It's no use writing a letter asking for an explanation. This boy has seen something, or he thinks he has, and the easiest way to find out just what that was is to go and see him.'

'So you're going to Shingleton?'

'Right away. Why not? It isn't far. I should be there by lunchtime, having had a bite of something to eat on the way. Do you feel like coming?'

'Of course. There's nothing much on at the moment.'

'All right. Look up Shingleton in the AA Guide and bring the car round while I scribble a note to the others to let them know, when they come in, where we've gone.'

'I'll do that,' said Ginger.

It turned out that Biggles had underestimated the time it would take to get to the address from which the boy had written, although admittedly they stopped on the way for lunch. The task of finding the house, Marsh Cottage, was not made easier by the fact that there was no actual village of Shingleton, as had been supposed. The name covered a district of cottages, mostly the homes of farm workers, scattered over an area as rural as could be found even in thinly populated regions of East Anglia. This meant frequent stops to ask the way.

However, eventually they found themselves in a lane, little more than a track, which they were assured by a man cleaning out a ditch would take them to the house they sought.

It was well named, for it stood alone on the marginal ground that lay between cultivated farm land and a broad expanse of flat, reed-covered salt marsh that ended on a bleak foreshore of the North Sea. It was in fact a landscape typical of many remote areas of the East Coast. There was little to break the drab monotony of coarse, tussocky grass and rushes. The tower of some distant church stood stark on the horizon.

A derelict windmill raised a gaunt and tattered arm to heaven. A small herd of black cattle gazed near a straggling wood of dwarf, wind-bent trees.

'Our young friend would certainly get a wide view from here, if this is where he lives,' observed Biggles as he brought the car to a stop at a short path leading to an old thatched cottage. The track, treeless, wandered on a little way to lose itself in the saltings.

They got out, the slam of the car doors bringing from the back of the house a middle-aged woman whose expression of surprise suggested that visitors were an unusual event.

Biggles raised his hat. 'Good afternoon, ma'am. Is this Marsh Cottage?'

'It is,' was the reply, given somewhat curtly.

'Would you be Mrs Stone?'

'Yes.'

'Is Robin at home?'

The boy's mother frowned, planting her hands firmly on her hips. 'What's he been up to now?' she demanded.

'Nothing to worry about,' Biggles hastened to assure her. 'You speak as if he was in the habit of getting into mischief,' he prompted.

'He wastes too much time over things that don't concern him.'

'I see. Well, we're police officers. He wrote a letter to us hinting that he had something to report.'

'So that's it. I knew he was up to something. I told him to mind his own business.'

'I wouldn't talk like that, Mrs Stone,' reproved Biggles gently. 'I'm sure you have an intelligent son, in which case you should encourage him in what he thinks is the right thing to do. Is your husband at home?'

'No. He's cutting reeds on the marsh. That's his job.'

'And where's Robin?'

'Gone to school. He should be on his way home by now.'

'Have you any idea why he wrote to us?'

'No; unless it's something to do with planes. He's got planes on the brain.'

Biggles smiled faintly. 'He might do worse than that. Which way does he come home?'

'Up the lane.' The woman pointed. 'As you go back you should meet him. He has a two-mile walk.'

'Thanks,' acknowledged Biggles. 'We'll do that. By the way, I hope you won't scold him for writing to us. Whatever he may or may not have seen, I'm sure he acted for the best; and our job would be easier if there were more boys like him to keep an eye on things. We can't be everywhere.'

Mrs Stone relaxed a little. 'Well, I suppose there ain't much here for him to do except watch for planes going over. It used to be birds he watched. Now it's planes. He knows 'em all. Keeps 'em all written down in a book.'

'Does he, though? I must ask him to show me that book some time. We'll go to meet him. You won't mind if we keep him talking a little while?'

'He comes home any time he likes. Stands staring at the sky half the time.'

'Good. Thank you, Mrs Stone. Good afternoon.'

The woman retired. Biggles turned the car and drove slowly back along the track.

They hadn't far to go. They had covered perhaps half a mile when they saw a rather small boy coming towards them, a satchel over his shoulder, swinging his

149

cap. He stopped when the car, drawing level with him, pulled up. Two bright eyes in a freckled face regarded the occupants with frank surprise and perhaps a little suspicion.

'Is your name Robin Stone?' enquired Biggles, getting out.

'Er—yes, sir,' was the answer, after a brief hesitation.

'The very chap I want to see. My name's Bigglesworth. I'm a detective. You wrote me a letter — remember?'

Robin flushed — a natural reaction to surprise and excitement. 'Of course I remember. Have you come all the way from London to see me?'

'Of course. Now sit down on the running-board beside me and tell me all about it.'

'It's about a plane.'

'Yes, I understood from your mother you take an interest in planes.'

'That's right,' confirmed Robin. 'I used to go in for bird watching. That's how I began to notice the planes going over. Where I live there's nothing much else to look at.'

'I can believe that,' agreed Biggles.

'Now I know all the regular planes that go over. I reckoned to tell the time by them, but you can't always do that because sometimes they're later on account of the weather. I know when they're likely to be late. I can't always see 'em, but I can hear 'em; and I can tell most of 'em by the noise the engines make.'

'Splendid. I call that an interesting hobby. Do you know the names of the planes?'

'Some. Not all. A boy at school lent me a book on how to tell planes by the shapes and the marks they have on them. I write them down – that is, any new ones I see.'

'Was it one particular plane that made you write to me?'

'Yes. That's right.'

'Tell me about it. Was it one of the regulars?'

'No. It was a new one to me.'

'Is that why you noticed it?'

'Partly. But really because it was flying so low.'

'Which way did it come from?'

Robin stood up and pointed towards the sea. 'That way. It came in over that hump, which is a big heap of shingle. It kept straight on and disappeared over there.' Again he pointed. 'Straight towards the old windmill.'

'Could you see any marks on it?'

'No. It was only just getting daylight, and a bit misty, but I would have seen marks if there had been any because it was so low. I was dressing when I heard it coming. I ran out to the back of the house and watched it go past. Its wheels were down and I thought for a minute it was going to land; but if it did I didn't see it.'

'Could you describe this plane?'

'Not really. It was a high-wing monoplane. It had a thick cockpit with two engines, one on each side; but I can tell you this: it wasn't a jet. I can always tell a jet. Oh yes, and it seemed to have two tails.'

'Did you see it come back?'

'No. But it might have done when I was in school. That was the first time I saw it.'

'Do you mean you've seen it again since?'

'Yes. The same time on Tuesday morning, flying in the same direction. It was what it did then that made me write to you. I posted the letter to you the next morning on my way to school.'

'What did it do?'

'As it went over the wood it dropped something. Either that or a piece fell off it.'

Biggles threw Ginger a significant glance and went on: 'What did this thing look like?'

'It looked like a bundle, a pretty large one.'

'Did you go to see what it was?'

'No.'

'Why not?'

'Because of the bull.'

'What bull?'

'There's been a bull out there with the cows. He's fierce and won't let you go near 'em. He's chased me more than once. They usually keep near the trees.'

'Who do the cattle belong to?'

'A farmer named Mr Werner. He has grazing rights. His place is about two miles past the wood.'

'Do you know him?'

'No, but I've heard talk of him.'

'What sort of talk?'

'Well, the boys say he's a bad-tempered man and carries a stick. He won't let anyone on his land.'

'I see. Tell me this, Robin. Was the plane flying low when this bundle fell off it?'

'Only just over the trees.'

'And you thought I ought to know about it?'

'Well, I thought there was something not right about a plane flying so low and dropping things off it.'

'Did you see the plane go back?'

'No. I haven't seen it since.'

'Did you notice anyone near the wood when this happened?'

'No. But I can't think of anyone who would be likely

to go near the wood. There's nothing to go for. Boys keep away on account of the bull. Some time ago I used to go there bird watching, but it's so boggy I always got my feet wet.'

'Do you happen to know if the bull is still there?'

'I looked this morning on my way to school, but I couldn't see him. But of course he might be inside the wood.'

'Did you tell your mother about this strange plane?'

'Yes.'

'What did she say?'

'She told me to mind my own business and get on with my lessons. She isn't interested in planes.'

'Did you tell the local policeman?'

'No. I haven't seen him lately. He comes round on a bike once in a while. I don't suppose he knows much about planes, anyway.'

Again Biggles smiled. He got up. 'I wonder if the bull is still there. If he isn't we might have a look to see if we can find this thing the plane dropped. Can you spot him, Ginger?'

They all stood on the running-board of the car and explored the marsh with their eyes. 'I can't see him,' said Robin. 'He doesn't go far from the cows and they're some way from the wood now.'

'Can you remember the spot where the thing fell?' asked Biggles.

'I could go straight to it. It was towards this end nearest to us.'

'Then I think I'll go and have a look round. Robin, you'd better go on home.'

Robin looked disappointed. 'Can't I come with you?'

'What about the bull?'

'I can run. He doesn't follow you far.'

Biggles hesitated. 'All right. But you be ready to run – and don't tell your mother what you've been doing or she'll be after me.'

'I know when to keep my mouth shut,' declared Robin.

Keeping close together, watching for the bull, they set off for the nearest point of the wood, a distance of perhaps a hundred yards. It could soon be seen that the trees were not so much of a wood in the generally accepted meaning of the word as a straggling belt of willows, birch and alder, all of which like to have their roots in water.

The bull did not appear. The cows took no notice of them, so the wood was reached without alarm or interference.

'The thing fell about here somewhere,' said Robin, and the hunt began.

It went on for some minutes. Then Biggles stopped suddenly and put a hand on Robin's shoulder. 'I think you ought to be getting along home, now,' he said. 'Your tea must be ready, and I don't want your mother to blame us for keeping you out.'

'All right, sir,' agreed Robin reluctantly. 'But you'll let me know if you find anything?'

'Of course. We'll see you again.' As Robin turned away Biggles went on, speaking seriously: 'I want you to promise me something.'

Robin's eyes opened wide. 'Yes, sir.'

'Don't tell a soul what you've told us, and don't tell anyone we are here or what we're doing.'

'I understand. I promise. I hope I haven't wasted your time.'

'Don't worry about that,' returned Biggles. 'You were absolutely right to report what you'd seen, and you deserve full marks for using your head.'

Robin flushed with pleasure and went off.

Biggles watched him until he was clear of danger from the bull, should it be in the vicinity, and then turned to find Ginger looking at him curiously.

'What's the idea, sending him off like that?' asked Ginger.

Biggles answered: 'There's something here it would be better for him not to see.' He took a pace forward and pulled aside a handful of osiers to reveal what lay beyond.

No further explanation was necessary. It was the body of a man, half buried in the soggy ground.

'So *that's* the bundle that fell from the plane,' breathed Ginger, after his first gasp of horror.

Biggles walked slowly round the dead man. Once he stopped and stooped to examine something closely. He did not touch the body.

It was that of a youngish man, fair and good-looking. He wore a suede jacket with a fur collar, corduroy trousers and sheepskin-lined ankle boots. On his hands were oil-stained gloves, but his head was bare.

Straightening himself, Biggles said: 'There was one thing wrong with what you just said. He didn't *fall* from the plane. He was thrown out.'

'How do you know?'

'Because he was already dead. At least, so we may suppose, since a man who has been shot through the back of the head from close range doesn't live long. This is no accident, Ginger. This is murder. Had it not been for young Robin the body could have lain here for years before it was found. Perhaps never. As it is, it can only have been here for a couple of days. Robin told us he saw something fall from a plane on Tuesday. He posted his letter to us on Wednesday. We got it this morning, Thursday.'

'Robin also said the plane came in from the sea. Doesn't that strike you as queer? I mean, why throw out the body here? If someone in the plane was so anxious to be rid of it why didn't he dump it in the sea?'

Biggles nodded. 'You make a point there. There must have been a reason for that. Without having had time to give the matter much thought I can think of one possibility. From the way he's dressed this man was either a pilot or air crew. An ordinary man doesn't walk about the streets in such clothes. Look at the oil stains on the gloves, and the shoulder of the jacket. There must have been at least one other person in that plane, anyhow, another pilot, or it would have crashed. It flew straight on. After all, no man in his right mind would shoot his pilot unless he was able to take over control himself. I can't see a man pushing a body out of a plane and at the same time keeping it under control. I'd say there were two other men in that plane.'

'I don't get it. If murder was intended, and it must have been, why did they wait till they were here?'

'Maybe the other pilot didn't know where they were going. He could have waited to find out. Once over the coast on a straight course was as much as the murderer wanted to know. Fortunately we know from Robin just what that course was. The big heap of shingle, the wood and the windmill would be conspicuous landmarks.'

'True enough. Another thing that puzzles me is this. This chap was shot from behind. That means the two pilots couldn't have been sitting side by side, as you'd expect.'

'It could be that this man, assuming he was a pilot and at the joystick, didn't know he had another pilot on board. There must have been enough room in the plane to move about. Pity Robin couldn't identify the type. The fact that it carried no markings suggests it was up to something illegal. It didn't want to be recognised.'

'Then why fly so low?'

'The obvious answer to that would be to keep under the radar screen. We've had no report from radar for weeks of an unidentified plane crossing the coast, so apparently it did that. We know from Robin where it came in, but how far it went inland when it got here is another matter. It might have been only a mile or two; it might have been a hundred. Robin hasn't seen it go back, so there's a chance it may still be here. His description of it isn't very helpful.'

'A twin-engined high-wing monoplane with a big forward compartment and a double tail sounds like a freight carrier. Does that suggest anything to you?'

'The only machine I can think of that fits – ruling out home-built aircraft – is the new job being developed at the Wolfschmitt Works in East Germany. I've never seen one, but I read the preliminary report of the trials. Anyhow, it's safe to reckon the aircraft came from abroad, from somewhere in Europe.'

'If you go through this man's pockets that might tell us something about him.'

Biggles shook his head. 'You may not have realised it, but we're in a bit of a spot. If we touch the body the county police may not thank us for interfering. This is a case of murder. The body will have to go to the mortuary for a post-mortem examination. It means an inquest, and that unfortunately will be reported in the newspapers; which is a pity, because the man, or men, responsible for this will learn that the body has been found, and that'll put them on their guard. I'd rather they didn't know, but without causing trouble I don't see how it is to be avoided.'

'Does that mean we shall have to drop the case?'

'Not necessarily. There's no reason why we shouldn't proceed with what we came here to do, which is track an unidentified plane behaving in a suspicious manner. If we're to find it now we shall have to be quick about it.'

'What can we do?'

'Fly over the course tomorrow morning early looking for anything that might give us a lead.'

'The plane may have gone home by then.'

'I realise that. We could ask young Robin to keep his eyes and ears open for it. But we'll deal with that later. The first thing we must do is report this to the local police. The nearest town is Sandstreet. It's about twelve miles from here. I'll wait while you slip along and report to whoever is in charge.'

'What shall I tell him?'

'You'll have to be a bit cagey about that, or he'll want to know what the devil we're doing in his district. Don't say more than is necessary. Tell him who you are. Don't mention Robin. Say we were following up a clue involving air smuggling – which is true enough – and this is what we found. There's nothing irregular about that. Say I shall do nothing till he gets here. He can go through the dead man's pockets, although I doubt if he'll find much. If, as it seems to me, this was a carefully planned job, the murderer would hardly fail to remove anything by which his victim could be identified.'

'Is that all?'

'It won't be necessary to bring a doctor. What will be needed is an ambulance and some strong stretcher bearers to carry the body to the road. Be as quick as you can.'

'When you've handed over do we go home?'

'Of course. I can't see any point in staying here. Besides, I want to be in the air tomorrow morning as soon as it's light enough to see what we're doing.'

'Okay. I'll press on.'

'If you see young Robin hanging about, watching from a distance as he may be, tell him to go home and stay there. His job is to watch for the plane.'

'I'll do that.' Ginger departed.

Biggles watched him as far as the road and saw the car move off. The cattle, still grazing peacefully, had moved further away. There was no sign of the bull. Then, finding a wind-blown tree, he sat on the stump. There was little he could do. He noted a broken branch above the body where it had crashed through before striking the ground. That was all.

He had been sitting there for the best part of an hour, deep in thought, with the light beginning to fade, when he was brought to his feet by a strident bellow. He knew what had produced it. Keeping under cover, he hastened to the edge of the wood on the side from which the noise had come. From there he saw the bull. It was ambling towards the cattle apparently having just arrived on the scene.

From where had it come? Biggles' eyes, roving swiftly over the landscape, found the answer. A van with tall sides, such as is used for transporting animals, was moving off inland, away from the marsh. It was too far off for him to see the number plate, but he noted the colour, dark green. It was either a new vehicle or had recently been painted.

The next question that came automatically was, why had the bull, which had not been there at the time of his arrival, been put back with the cattle? Was there any significance in that? It would now certainly keep people away from that area of the marsh. Was that the purpose? The animals were at a safe distance from him, so having no further interest in them he was returning to the body when a hail took his eyes in the direction of the road.

There he saw three vehicles standing. They were an ambulance and two cars, one of which he recognised as his own. Men were getting out, and from their hesitation to advance they had obviously seen the bull. However, they soon came on, walking at a brisk pace with their eyes on the danger, which appeared not to notice them. Ginger led. Then came two uniformed police officers. These were followed by two men carrying between them a rolled-up stretcher.

Biggles waited for them to join him, when Ginger quickly introduced the police as Inspector Carlow and Sergeant Brown. Both were big, healthy-looking countrymen. For a moment or two they gazed at the body.

Said Biggles: 'Naturally, you'll be wondering what brought us here, so I'll tell you.'

'I understand you're special police from the Air Section at Scotland Yard,' returned the inspector.

'Correct. We had a tip-off that an unidentified plane had been seen more than once over this part of the

160

coast, so we came along to check for places where an unauthorised landing might be made. There seemed no point in worrying you about it, and anyway it called for aviation specialists. We're pilots ourselves.'

'I understand that,' replied the inspector, in a friendly voice.

'Frankly, I wasn't expecting anything like this, and my first thought of course was to let you know,' went on Biggles. 'It's now up to you to take what action you think necessary. I haven't touched anything, but I hope you'll let me have any information you pick up which might help me to trace the plane from which this poor devil was thrown.'

'You say it's murder.'

'Couldn't be anything else. The man was shot through the head, so his body must have been put overboard.' Biggles smiled wanly. 'You find the murderer. I'll find the plane. Between us we might find both.'

'Do you know anything at all about this man?'

'Not a thing. I've never seen him in my life. I know no more than you. I've had a look round. There are no footprints, so it's reasonable to suppose no one has been here since the body landed. You can see the wound in his head. From the scorching of the hair I'd say he was shot from a distance of inches. You can see from the way the body has gone into the soft ground that it must have been dropped from a height. It came through this tree, smashing some branches.'

The inspector shook his head. 'This is a new line to me. It comes to something when bodies start dropping out of the sky. Have you got any theories?'

'None. There's the body. The man who dumped it

there could be half-way across the world by now. I said could be. Planes don't leave tracks, so we don't know where he went.'

'That's what I was thinking. Where do I start looking for a clue?'

Biggles shrugged. 'You might find something in his pockets that would tell you who he is and where he came from. Not that that would be much help if the plane was a foreigner.'

'Well, I might as well take the body and see what I can make of it,' decided the inspector, without enthusiasm. 'What are you going to do?'

'As far as I can see at the moment all I can do is fly over in the morning and look for traces of the plane.'

'I wish you luck,' returned the inspector. 'The air seems a queer place to look for traces of anything.'

'You never know what you might see from the air,' answered Biggles. 'A plane can't stay in the air all the time. Eventually it has to come down. And where it comes down it sometimes makes a mark. I can cover a lot more ground from the air than you can on the ground.'

'Yes, I reckon you can,' conceded the inspector. 'What would you be looking for?'

'The plane. Possible landing grounds. Wheel tracks in the grass.'

The inspector looked incredulous. 'Do you reckon to find 'em?'

'One never knows. I may not have to look far.'

'How do you work that out?'

'The plane that unloaded this body didn't want to land with it on board. It must have been in a hurry to get rid of it. That suggests it hadn't much further to go.

Have you ever been up in a plane, Inspector?'

'No, I can't say I have.'

'Would you like to?'

The inspector looked surprised. 'With what object?'

'To have a look at your territory from a new angle. I was thinking; you know the district better than I do. I shall be along in the morning in a police helicopter. I could pick you up. You could tell me who lives where, and so on.'

'Yes, I could do that. Where would you pick me up?'

'Here. Say, about daybreak. Five-thirty.'

'I'll be here.'

'Fine.'

'Now I'd better be getting along.' The inspector turned to the stretcher bearers. 'All right, you fellows, get him to the ambulance.'

As they all walked to the road Biggles said: 'If you find anything of interest in the pockets you can tell me in the morning.'

'I'll do that.' The inspector kept glancing at the bull. It was looking at them, but it did not move. 'What's that damn bull doing here?' he muttered.

'Keeping people at a distance, maybe,' answered Biggles lightly. 'Do you know who it belongs to?'

'Must belong to a feller named Werner. He farms all this land. Why?'

'Nothing much, except that we shall be flying over his ground in the morning.'

The inspector looked hard at Biggles, but he said nothing, probably because they had now reached the road.

There they parted, with the police following the ambulance, and Biggles and Ginger cruising along

163

behind. It was nearly dark.

'Did you see Robin?' asked Biggles presently.

'Yes. As you suspected, he was watching from a distance, behind some rushes. I had a word with him. I told him we had found the thing that fell off the plane, but I didn't say what it was.'

'Anything else?'

'I told him to go home and stay there. I said his job was to watch for the plane. If he saw it, or heard it, he was to run to the nearest phone and tell us. I gave him our number. I also said we might fly over in the morning. If we did a circle near his house he'd know it was us.'

'Good.'

'Have you any ideas?'

'One or two, but they're pretty vague.'

'Where did that bull suddenly come from?'

'That's one of the things I'm hoping to find out. All I can tell you is it arrived in a green cattle truck. There may be nothing to it, but it would be an effective way to discourage people from going near that wood.'

'I see what you mean,' returned Ginger slowly. 'What was the idea of asking the inspector to come with us in the morning?'

'In the first place, as I said, he knows the ground. Then again, we shall be operating over his district. And finally, there's just a chance we may need help. I have a feeling that that plane, if it's still here, isn't far away. According to Robin its wheels were down, presumably ready for landing. Nor have I forgotten that one of the crew carries a gun and doesn't mind using it; for which reason I shall carry one myself tomorrow. You'd better do the same.'

The following morning, at the appointed time, the air police helicopter dropped lightly on the marsh close to where Inspector Carlow's car stood on the track. The inspector and Sergeant Brown had got out and stood waiting. There had been no message from Robin, so it was assumed he had not seen the mystery plane.

The weather was fair, one of those quiet, still mornings that promise a fine day, although at the moment visibility was not as good as it might have been on account of a slight ground mist that hung over the damp ground. This, it could with confidence be supposed, would soon be dispersed by the rising sun.

'Well, did you find anything interesting on the body?' was Biggles' first question to the inspector.

'Nothing to shout about. We have the bullet. It was lodged in the skull. There was nothing in the pockets, so they must have been emptied by the murderer, which makes identification practically impossible. We think the man was a German. Anyhow, his clothes were made of German stuff.'

'Have you told the press about this?'

'Not yet. I thought it would be better to wait till we've had a look at things.'

'Quite right. What you tell me suggests, although it doesn't prove, that the plane came from Germany. Well, let's get on. I can't take you both, but I'll tell you what, sergeant: I shan't travel fast, so there's no reason why you shouldn't follow us, or keep an eye on us, from the road.'

This was agreed.

'What exactly are you going to do?' the inspector wanted to know.

'First I shall fly out over the sea a little way and then

come in following the natural landmarks, which is what the pilot of a small civil aircraft, not on a scheduled flight, would probably do. That windmill, for instance. Of course, it can't be guaranteed, but I hope by doing that to be on the same course as the plane we're looking for. It would be expecting too much to hope to see it, so all we can do is look for signs of it; by which I mean a field in which it could have landed or a building large enough to house an aircraft. If it's still here it could be camouflaged, so watch for anything that looks unusual or out of place. We might see wheel tracks. Those of an aircraft are usually wider than those of a surface vehicle and they begin in the middle of a field, not at the gate. With the dew still on the grass they should show up plainly from the air. You understand, Inspector, this is our job, and we've done it so often that we know the routine; but there's no reason why you shouldn't have a go at air spotting. I shall keep low. Tell me if you see a green cattle truck.'

'What's that got to do with it?'

'I don't know, but one was on the marsh yesterday and I saw nothing else moving.'

'I'll do my best,' promised the inspector, who seemed to be entering into the spirit of what for him was a novel operation. 'If you see anything suspicious what will you do?'

'Land and have a close look at it.'

The inspector looked worried. 'I've no warrant.'

'Don't let that worry you. If everything is as it should be no reasonable man would complain about the police doing their job. Only a man with something to hide, or be afraid of, would be likely to object. And by the way, as the man we're looking for has already got a murder on his hands, we can expect him, if we're lucky enough to find him, to be really nasty. Remember, he carries a gun. Now let's see what our luck is like.'

'Are you relying on luck?' questioned the inspector, dubiously.

'On a job of this sort one has to rely on it a little, but not entirely,' answered Biggles, smiling faintly. 'It's only fair to say that in a case like this we have advantages over you earth-bound coppers. We can see over a lot of ground at the same time. There are no obstacles in the air to get in our way, and we can move fast. Another thing that may strike you as odd, and this we have learned from experience: crooks who employ aircraft are not suspicious of other aircraft. Perhaps it's because they imagine that by using what to them may be a new form of transport they feel they're safe. They don't realise that coppers can fly too. Anyway, they take less notice of another aircraft than they would of a police car if it rolled up. But let's press on.'

Biggles got in and took over the controls. Ginger sat beside him. The inspector got in behind and the 'chopper' whirled its way towards a sky now showing patches of blue.

The machine first headed out to sea a little way and then, turning inland, took up a course over the pile of shingle in line with the windmill with the wood between. This took it near the back of Robin's home, and Ginger nudged Biggles when he saw a small figure in the garden, face upturned.

Biggles smiled, but all he said was: 'We shall have to give him a joy ride one day.'

The aircraft, at a height of never more than four hundred feet and proceeding slowly, flew over the now sinister wood and, beyond it, a strip of marsh. In front now stretched miles of typical, flat East Anglian countryside, some of it grassland, some under cultivation and some open heath of bracken with a sprinkling of silver birches. Most of it therefore could be ignored, and attention concentrated on and around the big pastures. A few of the fields were very large. Here and there was an isolated cottage. Standing on a slight knoll, over-looking a large, well-cropped meadow, although there was no stock on it, a red brick farmhouse with extensive outbuildings was conspicuous.

'That's Werner's place,' said the inspector, from behind.

'There's the green cattle truck in the yard,' added Ginger, and then grabbed the side of the machine to steady himself as the helicopter yawed steeply.

'By thunder! And there's the thing we're looking for,' snapped Biggles.

It is unlikely that no one was more surprised than he at that moment. Indeed, the way he spoke made that evident. Although he was looking for signs of it, the last thing he expected was to see the plane standing in the open. Yet there it was, near the farmhouse, close to the boundary hedge of the big field, with its airscrews flashing. This could only mean that it was about to take off.

What the inspector, unaccustomed to flying, thought of the next minute, we do not know, but it is likely that he thought his end had come. The machine went over on its side, straightened, and then dropped – well, fast, if not quite like the proverbial stone.

There was no time for explanations – not that any were necessary as far as Ginger was concerned. He

168

realised as well as Biggles that if the aircraft below them got off the ground they would have no hope of catching it. The only way to prevent that from happening was to block it, to land close in front of it.

This is what Biggles did, putting the helicopter on the ground within fifty feet of its nose. 'Come on, Carlow,' he shouted, and flinging open the door jumped out.

Simultaneously two men sprang out of the other plane.

What Biggles had said about aircraft not being associated with police was demonstrated when one of the men shouted furiously: 'Fool. What are you doing?' making it clear that he had not grasped the situation.

Biggles quickly disillusioned him. 'We're police officers and I have some questions to ask you,' he announced curtly, striding forward.

The appearance of Inspector Carlow, who was of course in uniform, must have confirmed this.

The two men reacted swiftly. One started to run. Ginger dashed after him. Biggles made for the other who, seeing him coming, snatched an automatic from his pocket and fired. But Biggles, seeing the weapon, had jumped sideways and drawn his own. 'Drop it,' he rapped out. The man hesitated. He looked round for his companion, and seeing him on the ground with Ginger on top of him, shrugged and threw down the pistol.

The inspector, his expression grim, walked forward and snapped handcuffs on his wrists. 'You'll be sorry you did that,' he growled.

At this moment the police sergeant, who must have kept in close touch with the helicopter in his car, came racing across the field. He gave Ginger a hand with his prisoner, who was still trying to resist. Handcuffs put an end to that.

Biggles returned his gun to a pocket and looked at the inspector with a queer smile. 'You see what I meant about luck,' he said dryly. 'Another minute and this machine would have been away. You need more than brains to judge things as fine as that.'

The inspector nodded. 'What now?'

'You've got your prisoners. I'm putting their aircraft under arrest. You could help me by posting a constable to guard it until I get instructions from my Chief as to what he wants done with it.'

'I'll do that. Now I'll get these two characters along to the station.'

'Before you go, stand by for a minute while I see if they were taking anything away with them.' Biggles advanced to the aircraft and opened the cabin door. He stopped, staring. Then he turned and beckoned. 'Come and look at this.'

A man, bound and gagged, was lying on the floor.

'Great Scott!' gasped the inspector.

'You know him?'

'Yes. It's Werner, the farmer. What the devil . . . ?'

'Let's get him untied and perhaps he'll tell us the reason for this,' suggested Biggles practically.

The farmer was freed. 'Thank you,' he said calmly.

'What was the idea of this?' enquired the inspector.

'They were taking me to Germany,' answered Werner simply.

The inspector took a photograph from his pocket. It was an after-death portrait of the murdered man. 'Do you happen to know who this is?' he asked.

Werner's face turned ashen. His eyes filled with tears. He bowed his head. 'It's my son,' he said

170

brokenly. He looked at the two prisoners. 'You devils!' he grated. Then he sank down with his face in his hands.

Said Biggles quietly to the inspector, 'You'd better give him time to get over it. He can tell you all about it later. There's no immediate hurry. I'll leave it to you.'

'What I don't understand is how you got on to this business in the first place,' said the inspector, looking puzzled.

'I told you I had a tip-off.'

'Yes. But from whom?'

'You'll be surprised. Do you know a house, near the wood where we found the body, known as Marsh Cottage?'

'Yes. It's the last house down the lane.'

'That's right. It's occupied by a man named Stone.'

'I've seen him about. Cuts reeds for thatching, I believe.'

'He has a son named Robin, a boy of thirteen.'

'What about him?'

'He was the tip-off.'

'You're kidding.' The inspector looked incredulous.

Biggles went on. 'Some boys collect the names and numbers of locomotives. Some collect car registrations. Robin is right up to date. He collects planes. A stranger went low over his house, twice. He wrote to me saying he thought I ought to know about it. That's what brought me here.'

'Well! I'm damned! Why didn't he tell me?'

'And if he had, what would you have done about it?' challenged Biggles.

'You get me there,' confessed the inspector frankly. 'Nothing. I've plenty to do without listening to the tales of little boys.'

Biggles wagged a reproving finger. 'That's where you make a mistake. Little boys today have big eyes and keep them wide open. Some of them know what goes on as well as we do.'

'I'll remember it.'

'Which reminds me. I promised Robin I'd let him know the outcome of his information, and in view of what has happened I shall certainly do that. Now, while I'm on the spot seems as good a time as any. You may find his evidence helpful when this pair is brought to trial. We could do with more boys like him.'

'I'll have a word with him myself as soon as I've got these two inside,' declared the inspector.

Biggles looked at his watch. 'Don't be in too much of a hurry.'

'Why not? He won't have gone to school yet.'

'You won't find him at home. I have an idea that the reward he'd enjoy more than anything would be a joy-ride in an aircraft. If I'm right I'll give him one. He's earned it.'

'Meantime I'll see Werner and get his explanation of all this.'

'Good. I'll come along tomorrow to hear it. See you then. Come on, Ginger.' Biggles walked to the helicopter and took his seat.

It is hardly necessary to say that Robin got his joy-ride. Instead of looking up, he found himself for the first time looking down.

The whole strange affair was explained the following day when Biggles and Ginger saw the inspector in his office. Yet, in view of current events in Europe, it may

172

not have been so remarkable after all.

Mr Werner's story, which was unquestionably true, was this. He was a German who had been granted political asylum in England. Before that he had lived in East Germany, where he had been an engineer engaged on space research. He had defected to the West, changed his name and settled in Suffolk, where he had started a new life as a farmer, or, more correctly, a stock-breeder. The only person on the Continent who knew his address was his son, who had elected to remain in Germany because he was engaged to be married to a young woman there.

This son, who was a test pilot at the Wolfschmitt Works, had managed to keep in touch with him. He had been under pressure to reveal his father's address because the East German authorities had been anxious to bring him back to continue his research work. Seeing trouble ahead, he had recently let his father know that he was considering coming over to join him.

The secret police must have got wind of this, although the rest must remain conjecture. It seemed that two government agents, one of them a pilot, had got into his confidence with the object of getting his father's address. They must have suggested that they should all escape together, using one of the new Wolfschmitt aircraft. The scheme worked. The three of them had flown over together. After crossing the coast, Mr Werner's son must have revealed his objective, thus signing his death-warrant. The two agents, having got the information they wanted and having no further use for him, had shot him and thrown his body overboard. They would not want to land at Mr Werner's farm with the dead body of his son on board. This was Mr

Werner's theory of what must have happened.

We can now return to facts. He told the inspector of how the two agents, pretending to be friends of his son, had tried to persuade him to return to East Germany with them, saying that his son had decided not to leave Germany after all. Werner, suspicious, had refused, whereupon the men had resorted to force, and would no doubt have succeeded in their mission had it not been for the inquisitive eyes of young Robin Stone.

Biggles had been wrong about the reason why the bull had been put back on the marsh. It was in the hope of escaping from the agents that Mr Werner had put the beast in the truck and driven to the marsh. This had failed. The agents went with him and forced him at pistol point to return to the farm.

It only remains to be said that murder was proved against the two agents and they paid the penalty. Robin provided a vital piece of evidence by describing how he had seen the body fall in the wood, although at the time he did not know what it was. Ballistic experts were able to prove that the pistol carried by one of the agents was the same weapon that had killed Mr Werner's son.

So a rather dismal story ended. Thanks to the boy who watched the planes go by the Air Police were once more able to justify their existence.

If you have enjoyed this book you may like to read some more exciting adventures from Knight Books:

MORE EXCITING KNIGHT BOOKS

CAPTAIN W. E. JOHNS

☐ 10460 0	Biggles and the Plot that Failed	£1.50
☐ 33687 0	Biggles Breaks the Silence	£1.25
☐ 34513 6	Biggles Sees too Much	£1.25
☐ 34514 4	Biggles Forms a Syndicate	£1.25
☐ 34839 9	Biggles Works it Out	£1.50

ELIZABETH LEVY

☐ 28333 5	The Case of the Counterfeit Racehorse	95p
☐ 28585 0	The Case of the Fire-Raising Gang	95p
☐ 32793 6	The Case of the Wild River Ride	95p
☐ 32812 6	The Case of the Mile-High Race	95p

All these books are available at your local bookshop or newsagent, or can be ordered direct from the publisher. Just tick the titles you want and fill in the form below.

Prices and availability subject to change without notice.

KNIGHT BOOKS, P.O. Box 11, Falmouth, Cornwall.

Please send cheque or postal order, and allow the following for postage and packing:

U.K. – 55p for one book, plus 22p for the second book, and 14p for each additional book ordered up to a £1.75 maximum.

B.F.P.O. and EIRE – 55p for the first book, plus 22p for the second book, and 14p per copy for the next 7 books, 8p per book thereafter.

OTHER OVERSEAS CUSTOMERS – £1.00p for the first book, plus 25p per copy for each additional book.

Name..

Address..

....